NINE LIVES OF KAT

Copyright © 2023 Debbie Leanne Mant

Nine Lives Of Kat cover art © Bradley Francis Mant.

All rights reserved. No part of this publication may be reproduced or transmitted in any form or by any means without the prior permission of the copyright owner.

All characters and events in this publication, other than those clearly in the public domain, are fictitious, and any resemblance to actual persons, living or dead, is purely coincidental.

For Brad,

For all the love, support and endless encouragement to finally get Kat out into the world, all whilst being the most awesome human I've ever met.

And to Orville Peck, for providing the soundtrack I listened to relentlessly for the full two-year duration of writing Kat's story, special acknowledgment to Let Me Drown which I played more times while writing this book than I'll ever know, and Nothing Fades Like the Light, which, in my head, is the official track of Chapters 23-25

Nine Lives Of Kat

By Debbie Mant

Prologue

As I made my way home, passing through the shadows, I remembered being told how quickly you adjust to the shift in atmosphere after the night creeps into the village. The constant wailing of the sirens, tearing their way through the streets. The screeching of tires as the late-night workers, keen to get home, crossed routes with the boy racers, torturing their remodelled bangers in a vain attempted to make them the fastest. The all-night music blasting from the dishevelled student housing block on the corner, where it appeared to be one continual rave. It was true, I had become immune to it, walking alone was no longer something I dreaded, making me feel vulnerable and weak in a darkening whirlwind of lights, sounds and chaos, instead I found myself savouring the lonely, late-night journey, finding the night-time chorus almost a comfort now.

What was putting me on edge tonight was the noticeable absence of the usual evening soundtrack. No sirens, no screeching tires, no thumping bass pounding from the corner house. The deafening silence creating a menacing feel, as though any moment a lurking monster would appear from behind the eerie shadows and rip my little world apart.

I quickened my pace and found myself looking rapidly around, searching for the source causing the burning feeling that I was being watched. The echoing of my footsteps appearing louder each step and almost out of time with my own. Were they just my footsteps echoing? I couldn't be a hundred percent certain with myself now. The ominous sense of someone or something watching me from behind the shadows, mixed with the noticeable lack of the normal night-time village sounds was messing with my head. Something didn't feel right. The sudden roar of an engine as a car appearing from nowhere sped past me, causing the cat laying on the road to give a shrill wail as it jumped up, darting across in front of me, only to be instantly engulfed in a darkened alleyway a few metres down from my side. The paranoia setting in making me almost run now. I couldn't put my finger on it, but something was definitely off balance, and I needed to get home so I could breathe again. It was probably just my overactive imagination. In the usual busy sounds of commotion from the streets around me, I felt invisible, blending into the night, as though whatever I did or wherever I went wouldn't be noticed, just how I liked it. But in this eerie silence I felt vulnerable and seen, painfully aware that my world could unravel in the blink of an eye if only someone chose to pay the slightest bit of attention to me. Then they would all know the truth. The reality that the real monster walking these streets and turning the village upside down was me.

Chapter One

Thursday - Three Nights Ago

"Ok boys and girls, this is your final question." Alex boomed animatedly into the microphone. "So, get your glasses emptied now 'cause I'll be back behind that bar ready to take your orders again real soon." He added with a grin, flashing his whiter than white teeth, fully embracing his role as pub quiz host. The pub always had a regular crowd in, but the monthly quiz night Alex had started organising a few months back always brought in a decent amount more. They weren't exactly the enthusiastic, upbeat punters he was always holding out for, quite a contrast, the majority were so angry looking and intimidating that they made him downright nervous at times, but the possibility of winning some free drinks for the evening in the quiz made them, if only a little bit, more sociable and friendly than most other evenings, so Alex made the most of it.

"So, question fifteen, it's a toughie," He paused, raising one perfectly plucked eyebrow, "Who wrote the best-selling twenty fourteen novel Horrorstör?" He questioned with a knowing grin.

Generally, the quizzes were always pretty easy, general knowledge or alcohol related questions, but Alex loved to throw a curveball question in at the end, just to keep everyone on their toes. "Right then, get your answers down, your sheets in at the bar and your drinks ordered!"

Heading back to the bar himself, Alex noticed Kane waiting patiently, one elbow resting casually on the bar, beer in hand. Dark hair, immaculately combed as always, his gentle, dark brown eyes watching Alex as he walked over. Alex greeted Kane affectionately before making his way round the bar and pouring himself a rum and coke.

"Where did you find that question?" laughed Kat on Alex's return, emptying the glasses from the dishwasher tray back on to the shelves. "Honestly Alex, you're clearly far too knowledgeable for our little corner of the world, I don't think anyone's got one of your quiz final questions right since you started them, have they?"

"Well maybe if you hermits dared to venture further than the threshold of Smith Cove once in a while then you might just broaden those narrow horizons of yours and learn something new." Alex quipped back, laughing as he narrowly dodged a playful whack from Kat.

Alex had travelled pretty much everywhere over the past few years. When he met Kane in college, they made a bucket list of destinations they wanted to visit and had determinedly seen their plan through, making memories to last a lifetime, until almost a year ago, when they had returned to Smith Cove after hearing Kane's mum had taken a bad fall. They spent a fair few weeks helping her back to good health and in that stint, Kane realised how lonely his mum was since the passing of his dad a few years before and with Kane always travelling the globe. Alex missed their adventurous days but had settled surprisingly well into the comfort of a home life and he knew how much it meant to Kane to be sticking close by for his mum. The Wranglers Arms (more often than not, referred to as The Stranglers Arms) had rapidly become their favourite local waterhole and after Kat had befriended them both, she had convinced her boss that Alex's vast cocktail knowledge and jocular personality would be a great asset if they wanted to start bringing in some fresher crowds. He had recently taken on Jas, a twenty-four-year-old, dark-haired beauty, in the hope that she would attract some younger groups in, but her sharp tongue and permanent scowl hadn't had the desired effect. And while Alex seemed to hang out more on the customer side of the bar than actually serving, he did have a knack of getting even the tightest of customers to dig in their pockets a little more and the staff all took an instant shine to him, so as long as he was good for business, the boss was happy.

The pub goers had started to get their next rounds in and while Kat and Jas worked the bar, Alex casually filtered through the quiz sheets, tallying up the scores and announcing the winner of the fifty-pound drinks tab. It was a strategic move, taking it a little slower than needed, giving the punters plenty of time to get an extra paid round in before handing over the voucher.

"Looks like your quiz night brought in quite a crowd again?" Sarah observed to Alex when he joined her and Kane for a drink. "I've got to know though, what was the answer to that last one? The horror story one?"

Alex laughed and rolled his eyes, "Horrorstör, and it was Grady Hendrix, check him out some time, the guy's got some interesting stories to tell."

As the crowd from the bar finally dispersed, Kat made the most of the break in pulling pints and joined the others, while Jas disappeared out the front for a smoke. Kat was looking worn out from the busy rush. Her mousy, flyaway hair pulled back in a messy bun, her light brown eyes not as bright as usual and her smile, though never fully fading, weakening at the sides. She had been putting in double shifts the past couple of weeks, she needed the money, but the hours were taking their toll. This was her last of a six day stretch of double shifts and she couldn't wait to clock out tonight and have a much-needed day off.

"So where are you two planning on jetting off to next?" Kat probed Alex and Kane, "Somewhere exotic no doubt?" Though they had settled well into temporary home life in Smith Cove, they still liked the thought of dreaming about extravagant holidays abroad when they got a chance.

"Ah you know what, Kat," responded Kane, in a mock serious voice, glancing around the pub with his thick, dark eyebrows furrowed, "I couldn't think of anywhere we would rather be during this delightfully damp autumn than right here, with the calming sounds of police sirens and drunken singers in the streets, and the beautiful backdrop of dingy shops to browse away in, while the shop keepers glare at you like you're the biggest inconvenience to their day. What place on earth could possibly be more satisfying?"

Kat and Sarah laughed. It was true that their run-down village was considered somewhat less than desirable these days. "You know you'd miss it here the second you left!" Retorted Sarah, looking her usual effortless designer chic. Her tailored blazer teamed with jeans that probably cost more than Kat earned in a month, her long blonde hair perfectly tousled into the most delicate side plait, sipping daintily on her pinot grigio.

"You're not wrong." Kane smiled, his face relaxing once more, "There certainly is some strange charm in this little village, though god only knows what that charm is, but right now I really don't think I'd want to be living anywhere else."

"Well, I'm not entirely sure Jas is living her best life here right now." Alex added in a feign whisper, as Jas sulkily skulked back into the pub. "The sour face on her tonight, honestly, I've not seen her crack a smile since she got here!" He added, louder as Jas walked by, shooting him a look of daggers.

"Oh, be nice," laughed Sarah, leaning on the bar with Kane, "Maybe she's just having a bad day," She paused, watching Jas let herself through the door out the back to grab more bottles from the alcohol cellar. "I heard her on her phone out front when I came in, sounded like she was having a bit of an argument with someone, maybe she's started seeing someone, sounded like a guy on the other end of the line."

"Well let's hope she's friendlier to him than she is to any of us!" Kat retorted, "I tried talking to her about Jack the other night and she just rolled her eyes at me and said she's not interested in knowing everyone's relationship dramas. Seriously, how did she even get a job here, she's so stuck up and rude."

"Such a shame." Interjected Kane over the heightening sound of the usual pub atmosphere, where a fight was threatening to kick off at a table near the window. "She's a stunner and I thought she would fit in here great with you all at first glance, but her attitude stinks. There's only so many times you can make an effort to be friendly just to have her snub everyone who tries. Where is Jack tonight anyway? I noticed his mates have been here most of the night." He added, looking pointedly to the table teasing a brawl at any moment.

"I don't know actually," Kat replied, a little distracted, "I haven't heard from him much the past couple of days. I had hoped he would be in tonight just so we could clear things up a bit, I'm starting to think we're nearing the end of whatever me and him even is, but I really don't know. Maybe he's just got some stuff going on?"

For a slightly confused moment Sarah began looking around the pub before turning back to Kat, "Funny, when I was heading in a little while ago, I was sure I saw Jack hovering on his phone by the corner down the road, I guess it must have been someone else."

Once last orders had been called and the crowd started to die down, Kat took the opportunity to sneak out the back and try calling Jack again. They hadn't really had a proper argument, but something definitely felt off. He had seemed a bit distracted the past couple of weeks, and Kat hadn't been too worried, but the past day or two something had definitely shifted between them. It felt strained and awkward. Not how it was at the start. It was never a conscious plan for them to get together, it just kind of happened. They got on well, and whenever everyone was together in the pub or all hanging out back at the girls flat, Jack had been relaxed and flirty. It hadn't been too serious, and Kat was reluctant to put a proper label on whatever it was they had, but it was nice, and it made Kat happy. At some point though it had reached a level where people now saw them as a fully-fledged couple, and it seemed quite clear to Kat that being tied down was not what Jack wanted.

Kat had seen Jack a few times in the pub at the start, they had always chatted easily back and forth and knew each other fairly well before he first took her out. She had always been confident and could talk to anyone. Jack came in at least a couple of times a week, sometimes for a quiet drink and a game of pool with one or two friends, sometimes for big drinks and shots with a crowd, where they could be heard from halfway down the street. On those nights, more often than not Jack would at some point inevitably find himself outside, fighting with one of the other boys from his crowd. It was never over anything major, usually about some girl or a knocked drink and never causing any serious harm, just two men with too much alcohol and ego, by the end of the night they would be back round the same table again, drinking and laughing with the rest of the group as if nothing had happened. The only difference being that they would be sporting a black eye, or some cut knuckles. Nobody really ever took much notice, drunk scraps and noisy brawls were commonplace in Smith Cove.

Kat loved where she lived but nobody could pretend it was some picturesque, quaint little village, full of idyllic views and Stepford housewives. It was a village that seemed forgotten. Or maybe just nobody cared enough to try to change it from the dive it was known to have become. Petty crime was such commonplace now that it barely raised an eyebrow from the locals and loud music or angry rows well into the early hours were the norm. Despite the obvious negativity though, it felt, for a while, like her place in the world. Whether working the bar or being back in her and Sarah's flat across the road, it felt to Kat like she had finally found her gang and that for whatever reason, this is where she belonged. Little did she know that just a few short hours later she would be wishing more than anything that she had been anywhere else but here.

Chapter Two

Friday Evening - Two Nights Ago

Walking into the quiet apartment, Sarah instantly knew something wasn't right. She couldn't tie a specific reason to her feeling of unease, but the atmosphere felt wrong. Like something had been moved or someone had recently passed through the room and the dust had yet to settle again. Kat had left earlier than Sarah today, she had mentioned she was running a few errands out of town but maybe she had finished up early and was home already. As Sarah called her name in to the air though, with nothing but silence as a response, she felt sure Kat wasn't there. As she cautiously paced through the living room to check the kitchen, feeling her shoulders involuntarily tensing up at the eerie feeling caused by the unknown, Sarah tried to register all the surroundings, hoping that maybe her own absentmindedness as she rushed out to work that morning, leaving things out of their normal place, was actually all that was to blame for the unsettled atmosphere. The slightly askew sofa cushions she hadn't got round to plumping earlier, the cereal bowl still left on the coffee table from her rushed breakfast, keen to pinpoint what was out of place and put her overanxious mind at ease.

As she reached the kitchen, Sarah noticed the two bottles of pinot grigio, intended for her and Kat's girls' night that evening, still sat on the worktop.

"Shit!" blurted Sarah to herself, before stalking over and putting the wine back in to chill. She had pulled the bottles out from their chaotically filled fridge that morning while grabbing her lunch bag and smoothie from behind them. She had intended to put them straight back so they would be chilled and ready for the evening but had instantly forgot in her rush to get out the door.

Rolling her eyes at her own forgetfulness, but grateful she could put her feeling of something being wrong down to the wine being left out, Sarah felt her shoulders relax as she walked, much happier, towards her bedroom, keen to change out of her day clothes and into something more comfortable, ready for the much overdue girl's night in.

Untying her too tight hairband, allowing her thick blonde hair to cascade over her shoulders, Sarah was already switching off, excitedly mulling over in her mind all the gossip she had for Kat. It was only as she pushed open her bedroom door, remembering too late that she had left it open that morning, she felt the solid frame of a man rush past her from her room, too fast for her to notice any details about what he looked like or even what he was wearing, knocking her to the ground before everything went dark.

Kat and Sarah had shared the flat for a fair few months now. They had known of each other from around the village and seen one another in passing at the pub but they ran in different crowds and had never had an opportunity to get to know each other. It wasn't until Kat overheard Sarah one evening discussing her search for a roommate that Kat piped up. She had recently split from her ex-boyfriend and was currently sofa surfing from one friend's home to another until she could find somewhere permanent to live. Kat joined Sarah's table to discuss the spare room and by the end of the evening had agreed to move in that same weekend. Since then, Kat and Sarah had become firm friends. On the morning of Kat moving in,

Sarah felt a mixture of nerves, relief and excitement, she had been on the lookout for a roommate for a few weeks since moving in herself but being financially privileged enough to take her time finding the right fit, she had held off accepting anyone until now. The spare room was fully furnished, she just needed to find the right person with the right attitude to suit her dynamics. Sarah had a good feeling about Kat and Kat had seemed just as excited when hearing Sarah had a room to rent. Just trusting someone enough to share a home with was good enough for some but Sarah wanted someone she could chat to, laugh with, hang out with. As an only child and a wealthy one at that, Sarah had plenty of acquaintances but had never really found her place amongst friends, she wasn't shy and certainly wasn't a snob, but she always felt more of an extra with friends rather than a member of the main cast. What she really always wanted was a sister, a best friend who she could trust, share memories with, and be comfortable enough to be fully herself around.

Her apartment was ideal, two bedrooms, in a nice, for Smith Cove at least, new build block. The building had six apartments in total and had only been there a couple of months when Sarah moved in, by which point half of the apartments were already occupied. Sarah's, the flat next door to hers and one on the next floor up being the only ones remaining. Sarah never met the owner, but she had heard that he owned the entire block. By the time Sarah had arranged viewings, she heard on the grapevine that the flat next door was no longer available, though since moving in Sarah had never seen anyone coming or going or even heard any noise through the adjoining wall. She had formed the conclusion that it had probably been snapped up by some out of town rich guy, planning on using it as a secret location to hide his affair. Sarah wasn't complaining, at least with it being off the market and empty, there was no immediate risk of terrible neighbours moving it and disturbing her peace. She had heard the remaining apartment above her had also been snapped up around the time she moved in, Sarah heard the faint sound as the mystery resident moved around sometimes but as of yet she hadn't actually met them. It wasn't the sort of town where you would knock on a stranger's door just to say hello or to give them a 'welcome to the neighbourhood' box of biscuits or bottle of wine, you'd most likely be met with a "Fuck off!" and a slammed door. But Sarah loved her little space, making it the best it could look, filling it with her boho vibes, with throws and cushions covering every surface and the constant aroma of burning incense, or sometimes weed, filling her home.

With the sudden banging on the door signalling Kat's arrival snapping Sarah out of her reminiscent daydreaming, she took a breath and let Kat in. The nerves Sarah had felt, washed away in minutes. Kat seemed like the missing piece from the apartment, like it had been built just for her, and now it felt like home to them both.

"So now that I'm finally all moved in," Kat joked with a dramatic eye roll, "The important question is, do we head across to the pub to celebrate, or do we grab a couple of bottles from the offy and toast here instead?"

Sarah scoffed "Yeah them whole two bags you had seemed a real labour to move across, I honestly don't know how you managed it!"

Sarah had come from money, and though she had always tried to play it down, there was an ever-present air of luxury affordability to her. From her designer torn jeans to her gorgeous, shiny Gucci boots she wore everywhere. The financial difference between her and Kat though was never a factor. Deep down Sarah had always been a little embarrassed by her parents flashing the cash attitude and had been determined not to be so brash with her own money. She bought herself a little shop and turned it in to a gorgeous little boutique, selling treasures and trinkets shipped from all over the world. The money she brought in was barely a full wage, but she was happy and, combined with the monthly allowance check her dad had been insistent on sending her, still more than covered the monthly bills. While she was keen to stand on her own two feet and not be seen to always rely on daddy's money, the extra funds had definitely come in useful along the way, especially when bad days had come knocking and retail therapy was the only solution.

Sarah was the more glamorous of the pair for sure, with her perfectly shaped eyebrows, ever present false lashes and immaculately styled outfits, she was one of those lucky people who could throw any combination of clothing on last minute and still end up looking ready for the runway. She oozed style and confidence. Compared to Kat, who more often than not would be spotted in old jeans, doc martins and a plain tee, with her hair pulled up quick in a messy ponytail, usually running late. To most at first glance they would appear too different, and in many ways, they were the complete opposite ends of the scale to one another, but when they sat together in their flat, glass of wine in hand, the laughter and stories they shared were immeasurable.

They had impromptu parties from time to time, their flat was so close to the pub where Kat worked that it just made sense for everyone to file back to theirs once the pub door had closed of an evening. Sometimes just a few stragglers from their group, other times a whole pub full it seemed, even occasionally people they didn't even really know tagged along for the ride. Like when they finally met Lucas from upstairs, the mystery resident from the flat above theirs. Kat and Sarah had been standing with Alex, glancing round at the assortment of characters surrounding them, the last standing pub crowd who had made their way to the girls flat. A random guy had reached the pub just as they were locking up, they hadn't recognised him, but he looked so worn down and lost that Kat had pitied him and invited him to tag along with them all back to their flat. He was quiet and seemed to be lost inside his own head, like a stray pulled in from the rain, happy to be inside in the warm but unsure about whether he could trust his new surroundings. He was tall in a gangly sort of way, with mousey brown hair and glasses. Sarah was dismissive of him from the get-go, rolling her eyes and claiming he had a strange vibe, but Kat found herself glancing towards him over and over. Where had he come from? They hadn't even noticed him in the pub before, so maybe he was new to the village? It wasn't the quaint sort of village that anyone would opt to visit for a relaxed weekend retreat, more the type you would reluctantly pit stop in if you were having car troubles and had no option but to pull over, so unknown faces appearing was quite a rarity. Even Alex who knew everyone's business before they even knew it themselves hadn't ever noticed him in the pub. Jas had been working that night, but Kat saw her rush off when they locked the pub doors, so they couldn't ask her. Not that she ever gave much of a straight answer or more than the bare minimum response anyway.

Jas had worked with Kat and Alex for a while now, and though she was never specifically rude to Kat, she definitely gave a clear impression of keeping a distance. Like when Jack came in to meet with Kat at the end of one of her shifts a few weeks back, and Kat, trying to be polite and noticing Jas hovering awkwardly nearby, had attempted to bring her in to their conversation, Jas had down right turned on her heels and disappeared to clear tables, before leaving her shift early with a sudden migraine.

After a few minutes the curiosity surrounding the stranger got too much for Kat and she ventured over to try to find out a little about him or at least where he had appeared from.

"Hey again, thanks for joining us! I'm Kat, this is mine and my friend Sarah's flat. We've not seen you about before, have you just moved here or are you visiting someone, maybe?"

To Kat's surprise, up close he didn't appear almost nearly as gangly as he first seemed. His arms had the rugged definition of, maybe not someone who actively worked on their muscles at the gym, but perhaps someone who did a lot of manual labour, gaining accidental strength through their day-to-day routine. His eyes, hidden from afar by the reflection his glasses caused, up close now seemed dark and mesmerizing. He looked at Kat with an almost conflicted expression, before looking around at the others surrounding them. When he finally spoke, he seemed distracted and a little unsure.

"Hi Kat, it's a great apartment you've got here. I'm Lucas."

Throughout the evening Kat learned that Lucas was living in the flat above theirs, they had heard him moving around from time to time but never seen him. He said he was shy and didn't know anyone in the area and had been trying to build up the courage to venture over to the pub alone one evening, and how typical of him it was that when he finally did, it was closing time, and how nervous but appreciative he was to Kat for inviting him along to join the gathering.

Like most of the other locals, Lucas warmed instantly to Kat and was grateful for her reaching out to a stranger and making him feel like he belonged slightly more in this strange little village. From then on, though he still wasn't much of a chatter, Lucas became another regular in their pub full of misfits.

Which was where he had been that night, sat with his phone in hand, when the police had come barrelling in, speaking something quietly to Alex who was on the bar, before announced that a woman had been attacked and another was considered missing through abduction.

Chapter Three

Friday Evening – Two Nights Ago

Sitting by the grubby grey window, nursing my warm, scotch and coke, I find myself gazing out through the alcohol and tobacco smoke-stained glass, watching the raindrops on the other side, mirroring each other in their demise to the chipped paint covered frame below them. The sky outside, darkening over the past couple of hours through anger filled rain clouds as it crawled and drizzled towards nightfall, now nothing but a black hole, encompassing all the world outside of The Wrangler's Arms.

I make a conscious effort to pull my train of thought back to the present. The police have been here a while now, questioning everyone in the pub, desperate to find something, any little insight that could lead them to whoever has taken Kat, before it's too late. First impressions implied everyone seemed naturally full of concern, all rallying to suggest it must be an outsider, someone unknown to the village, but somewhere along the course of the last half an hour or so, there's been a shift. Sitting here observing the reactions and mannerisms of the acquaintances around me, I'm seeing people are getting suspicious, second guessing each other, finding plot holes in each other's overheard alibies. Up until now it's all been voluntary information, all seemingly wanting to assist in the search for Kat and the discovery of who has done this to her and Sarah, as well as the blatant rubberneckers just itching for further unsavoury details about what has actually happened to them, but the sudden reveal that they are packing up and returning to the station, preparing to start calling people in for official questioning has sent ripples through the pub crowd. Fingers are suddenly being pointed and accusations and gossip are now rife in the air.

That's the thing about Smith Cove, everyone is sceptical of those around them, nobody fully trusts one another because everyone here is hiding something. Secrets they want to keep hidden, a past, lies they hope will never come to light. But everyone is always so wrapped up in their own skeletons hiding in their closets that they miss the signs staring them in the face of the secrets that are kept by those drinking right beside them.

As I sit here, surrounded by those characters, the loud and obnoxious, the openly judgemental, the ones who think they are something better than this shithole town of ours, I allow myself just a moment of elation, feeling smug and invincible that not one of them can see what's right in front of their faces. I admit the initial plan derailed pretty quickly when the roommate got in the way, if she had stayed away then all this drama could have been avoided and it could have been put down to Kat just being AWOL, police wouldn't have batted an eyelid if it had been just a Smith Cove girl gone wondering, they certainly wouldn't have been searching for information here now, so I'm not entirely sure on my next move with Kat anymore, I'll have to be a bit more cautious, I hadn't prepared for such a large police presence to show up and the piqued interest now it's considered an abduction case has suddenly drawn more attention our way than I'd like, but I feel safe for now, nobody has even the slightest idea, they are looking in all the wrong places and beginning witch hunts for all the wrong people. I've heard my name muttered among the accused but so has pretty much every name in this pub, there's no real threat, at least not yet. I'll give my police interview when called to, and I'll play the part of the concerned Smith Cove resident as well as anyone else in this dumping ground of a village but I'll keep one step ahead.

I wished I could at least tell them she was safe though, and that I never originally planned to hurt her, but she just doesn't help herself. If only she would see that I'm doing it to help her. This isn't the path for her, she will just keep being treated like a fool and getting herself in more trouble if she carries on how she has been living. I'm doing what I'm doing to teach her, and look after her, if she would only listen and stop being scared. She is safe with me around, or at least safer than she would be without me here, and I want more than anything to keep her that way, but like others, I've grown tired of her lost puppy ways. Always trying to be everyone's saviour, thinking there's better in everyone, even the lost causes. I've seen how foolishly trusting she is over everyone around her, even welcoming everyone in to her own home, just so keen to be liked by everyone. It's pitiful and infuriating to see.

I've been watching her running herself in to the ground, I've seen how people treat her, take her for a fool. She thinks she's being nice, and that people are grateful but really, she is giving them all the ideal opportunity to take advantage, and I can't sit and watch anymore, her innocent trust in everyone is starting to make me angry. I had no choice but to take her, her actions before had brought all this on herself, but I want to help her and get her on the right track, I just wish I hadn't lost my cool, I didn't want to hurt her, at least not straight away, but she looked so disappointed and confused and angry when she saw me in her flat, why couldn't she have looked happy to see me? I felt betrayed and fury flooded though me, I snapped quicker than the bone in her leg did. I had planned it for so long, had been watching her, following her when needed, knew her inside and out, it should have been so easy. When it came to it though, she has been harder work than I expected. I thought I had gained her trust and she would do as she was told, but she didn't, she gave me no choice but to temporarily allow my more violent side to take the lead. I wasn't happy about it but if that's what it takes to get her to see what's right and learn where she keeps going wrong with her stupid games, then it will be worth it in the end, this stubborn behaviour is exactly why these lessons need teaching. If only the interfering flatmate hadn't of got home first, we could have saved so much unnecessary anger and stress for everyone. I didn't care if Sarah ended up hurt, it hadn't been part of my plan, but I'd certainly lose no sleep over it, she was an obstacle that needed removing, I did what I had to do, I acted swiftly, making sure she wouldn't wake up for a few hours, and left her in the flat. I had no use for her and dragging her along too would have been a problem I didn't need. If she gets in my way again though I'll have to be more assertive and remove her permanently.

Chapter Four

Friday Evening – Two Nights Ago

As the police cavalry finally left the pub, the tensions in the air ran high, a mixture of concern, panic and suspicion, putting everyone even more on edge, a vast contrast to the laid-back ambiance from the quiz evening the previous night. Alex and Jas had been requested to close the bar while the police presence was gathering all the information they could, so with them finally serving again, everyone swarmed to get a much-needed nerve relaxer.

"Jack, what did they say? Have you spoke to Kat today? I'm sure she was trying to call you a couple of times last night, I mean she didn't actually tell me she was calling you, but she kept disappearing on her phone and she said it had been a minute since she last heard from you?" Questioned Alex impatiently when Jack come over to order a double whisky.

Alex had never been a fan of Jack, the macho man, over the top, show off lout mentality had always been a red flag for him, after years of carbon copy bullies of the same calibre, regularly taking pleasure in beating the shit out of him for his confidence in being openly different to them. Jack had never been completely out of line to Alex, the usual drunk pub banter and the occasional comment maybe but Alex never had him pegged as anything more than just a bit of a cocky arsehole. He definitely hadn't treated Kat how she deserved, but to harm and abduct her? Alex just didn't know if he had it in him, though he was certain Jack was hiding something.

"I dunno man, maybe she was calling someone else?" Jack responded with a heavy sigh. "I don't remember her calling last night, and I definitely didn't speak to her. Maybe she's seeing someone? Like properly I mean, we all know me and Kat ain't nothing serious." Jack added, a little distractedly.

"Well, I think she always seemed a bit possessive of you, if you ask me Jack." Sniped Jas, bitterness and disdain dripping off her tone. "Maybe she's just gone off sulking somewhere because you stopped giving her the attention she was so desperately craving? I mean it's worked, hasn't it, if that's what she's done, now were all standing round talking about nothing but her!" Jas rolled her eyes irritably before walking off to serve the next customer.

"Yeah, let's be honest, she does take it all a little too personal, you know?" Jack remarked to Alex. "I'm sure she'll be back in here in a couple of days, probably just gone off in a huff somewhere." He added, necking his whisky before ordering another.

"You never did deserve her, Jack, do you know that?" Retorted Alex, growing visibly angry. "If Kat's just gone off willingly somewhere then how does that explain Sarah getting attacked too?"

"Does anyone know how we go about finding out how Sarah's doing?" Kane chimed in, eager to calm the growing tension between Alex and Jack.

"I tried calling her just after the coppers showed up but there was no answer, she was messaging me earlier today but hasn't responded since just after four thirty." Alex responded, pulling his glare away from Jack, "That tall copper told me she had been taken into hospital to be checked over and was still unconscious. I guess she's still at the hospital now and if she has woken up yet then maybe she doesn't have her phone." Concern apparent on his face,

"Hopefully she's awake already and will get out soon and can give us a bit of insight as to what the fuck's going on here, poor girl, hope she isn't too bruised up."

"Well, there's plenty of rats round here," Interjected Jack with a shrug, "So if anyone did see what actually happened then it's only a matter of time before they come crawling out to tell their tales." With that he picked up his glass and headed out the front door for a smoke, closely followed by Jas.

"God that guy gets under my skin." Alex stated out loud to nobody in particular. "You'd think he would be a bit more concerned. Even if he was cooling things off with Kat, you'd think he would still show a bit of decency, to her and Sarah, enough to care that they were safe at least!"

"I know babe, the guy's an arsehole, but try not to let him get to you. Seriously though, you don't actually think he could be involved in Sarah being attacked and Kat going missing, do you?" Kane questioned calmly.

Alex pondered momentarily, "I mean I want to say no, I can't see what he would gain from doing so and I don't think he's smart enough to cover it up if he had, but there's something off about him at the minute and he and Jas have definitely got some kind of secret they're keeping, she's not left him alone all evening."

"Yeah, I'd noticed that too. I know she's not keen on Kat or Sarah, hey let's be honest, they aren't that keen on here either, but you'd think Jas could at least pretend to show a little compassion or concern, if it is a random attack then it could have just as easily been her." Retorted Kane.

"Was it just a random attack though?" Alex questioned, thinking out loud, "I mean, I couldn't honestly think of anyone who would want to hurt our girls, Kat's genuinely the sweetest person, who would be evil enough to abduct her like that? And why? But I can't stop thinking about it all, how did the bastard even get into the building in the first place? Just seems there's more to it!"

"Hmm, I know what you mean." Agreed Kane hesitantly. "Let's hold off getting too Detective Drew about it though 'till we know a bit more. Hopefully we will hear from Sarah soon and she can enlighten us on exactly what happened. Who knows, maybe she even knows who the guy is."

Alex wasn't as diplomatic as Kane, with his calm approach to rationalising rather than throwing around accusations. Alex was adamant Jack was hiding something, whether he had a hand in Kat being taken or not, he still wasn't sure, but Jack had definitely been up to something he shouldn't be, so Alex felt Jack fully deserved the speculation and should expect every bit of judgement coming his way. Alex held off arguing his point further in that moment though, Kane's calm demeanour and ability to be level-headed in any given situation were part of what had attracted Alex to him in the first place, and in that moment Kane's lack of temper caused Alex's to mellow slightly in reflection, so he bit his tongue and let the subject lie, for now.

Chapter Five

Early Saturday Morning - Yesterday

As Sarah finally came round, squinting at the bright hospital lights blinding her, she could hear the muffled sound of people talking. Feeling fuzzy headed, she slowly lifting herself up on the bed, just enough to look around. She took in the image of two policemen, standing with a nurse. All three with furrowed brows. The nurse looked young and a little overwhelmed. Her Bambi eyes widening with innocence and panic as the older of the policemen was talking. Sarah wished she could hear what they were saying, but the normal hustle and bustle hospital noise, mixed with the infuriating beeping of the monitors she had somehow been attached to while unconscious made it impossible to recognize more than the odd few words.

"We are doing all that we can…we are looking everywhere for her…no visitors until we've spoke to her".

Sarah didn't understand, she may not have seen his face but the person who knocked her down was definitely a man, why would they say looking for 'her', did they suspect a woman of being involved in the robbery too?

She couldn't just lay here like this. As she prepared to pull herself up completely, the young nurse and both of the policemen headed in her direction.

"How are you feeling Sarah?" began the nurse in a careful, calm voice.

"Do you remember anything from the apartment?" interrupted the older cop. He didn't introduce himself, but his name badge visibly shared the information, DS Michael Williams. His greying hair and visible stubble suggesting a man who spent more time than most on the job, leaving little time to refresh at the end of the day. His blunt tone implying this was not someone who was messing around. He wanted information and he didn't have time to tip toe around for it. "If you could tell us everything you can recall, it is essential we have as many details as possible now".

"Of course I remember." I spoke, my voice groggy and muffled. I gratefully accepted the plastic cup of water the nurse was now holding out to me, before carrying on. "There was a guy in my apartment, he must have broken in somehow and was planning on robbing us, I guess I disturbed him, and he knocked me down as he ran out. I must had been knocked unconscious, which I guess is how I stayed until Kat came home and found me before she rang you. I didn't see his face and it all happened too fast for me to take in anything else about his appearance, so there's not really much else to say, and as you can see, I'm awake and fine now, so what I'd really like is to go home and forget this all happened. Is Kat here already?"

The Bambi nurse looked close to tears before catching Sarah's eye and plastering back on her serene nurse mask. Something wasn't adding up and Sarah was already losing patience.

Finally, the second cop spoke for the first time. He was definitely younger than the first, probably only been on the job for a couple of years, his eyes still looked like he believed there was good in the world and that he really could make the difference. He was tall and robotic in his minimal movements. His short brown hair sticking out here and there, rebelling against the excessive amount of product he had clearly used in a vain attempt to control it.

"Sarah, my name is DC Callum Haynes, we're extremely glad, and relieved, to see you awake, obviously you've been through quite the ordeal and I'm so sorry to have to put you straight on the spot and ask you this," He hesitated and swallowed back a lump in his throat, "But when you went in to your apartment, erm, did you see any…sign of a struggle? Anything out of place or broken?"

Looking confused and a little irritated Sarah shook her head, man that hurt, she could definitely do with some painkillers for that. "Look, like I said, the apartment was fine, nothing was out of place, the guy was hiding in my room, and he escaped past me as I walked in. If anything was broken then I'll just get it replaced, so I really wouldn't worry."

"Sarah, I'm afraid there seems to be a bit more to it than that. It wasn't Miss Carter who phoned us, it was a neighbour of yours, he heard a few loud crashing noises, and he came to check it out. The door was open when he arrived and there was no sign of a break in entry point, but a vase had been smashed and we found evidence of blood traces, which we feel may belong to Katherine, we also discovered a discarded handbag which had Miss Carter's belongings and I.D card inside. Your neighbour found you unconscious on your bedroom floor, with no sign of Katherine. We don't think this was a random burglary, we have reason to believe this was a deliberate attack and kidnap of Katherine Carter and that unfortunately you were just in the wrong place at the wrong time."

Sarah looked dumbstruck, all remaining colour draining from her already washed-out face, momentarily unable to process a response to the information being given to her.

"We are taking this case extremely seriously, but we do believe time is of the upmost importance if we hope to find Miss Carter safe. So, if you could tell us any information at all about any enemies Katherine has, or anyone that would wish her harm in any way? Anyone she may has been involved in an argument with? Even the smallest bit of information could give us a lead and help us get to your friend sooner."

Sarah sat, momentarily frozen, the overly bright hospital lights piercing into her eyes, the monotonous unrelenting beeping from the machines seemingly growing louder in her ears with every passing second. What they were saying just didn't make sense. Nobody would wish harm to Kat, she was pleasant to everyone, whether they deserved the decency or not, the wasters and creeps who occupied the pub booths night after night, or Jack, the amount of crap she puts up with from him messing her about and leading her on, and even Jas, the bluntness she dishes out and yet still Kat would try to be polite back, Sarah never knew how she had the tolerance to do it. She tried to rack her brain to piece together the chaos that was now in front of her. Who could be out to get Kat? If the police have said it was a deliberate attack, then it must be someone Kat knows so surely Sarah would know of them too? So why were they after Kat specifically and not her?

The Policemen were still talking at her, but Sarah couldn't take in what they were saying. She was busy scrolling though her mind of all the people they interact with. Maybe it was someone who had spotted Kat working a day shift, Sarah wouldn't have been around then so wouldn't have known. She needed to get out of this hospital bed and speak to Alex now!

"Have you spoke to anyone from the pub?" she abruptly interrupted the older officer's current monologue. "It's got to be someone who goes in there, Kat rarely goes anywhere else."

"We had a team of officers last night interviewing members of the staff and public over at The Wranglers Arms, if that is the pub you're referring too, but any specific names who you think could assist further would be greatly appreciated."

Sarah looked away for a few moments, brow furrowed and deep in thought, before something suddenly occurred to her, causing her eye to widen in horror. She remembered a couple of weeks ago having to loan Kat her key to have a replacement cut as Kat had somehow lost hers while staying at Jacks one night.

"Did you say there was no sign of a break in?" She questioned impatiently.

"That's right." DS Williams replied, ears pricked in hope of finding anything that might help the case.

"So, whoever it was must have let themselves in. You need to speak to Jack Stanford now!"

Chapter Six

Saturday Mid-Morning - Yesterday

Pacing the office floor, DS Williams impatiently waited for DC Haynes to finish arranging the afternoons interviews. He knew he wanted to get the boyfriend in first, Mr Jack Stanford, and the tall guy who worked the bar had volunteered to come in whenever needed, but hopefully they could fit a few more in today too. The more information they could collect quickly, the more efficient their search would become.

"Sir, I've arranged two interviews for this afternoon." DC Haynes announced as he entered the room. "DC Mills and DC Anderson are available to assist with interviews if needed. The number we had for Jack Stanford was unrecognised, so we are hunting out a different one. I've found a contact number for the sister of Katherine Carter though, a Mrs Hannah Payne, would you like me to call her now and inform her of the situation?"

DS Williams paused momentarily, mulling over the best course of action. He had been playing this game long enough to know that Kat's chances of even still being alive were pretty slim and even if by some miracle she was still breathing, the chances of them getting to her before the situation got worse were almost non-existent. He looked at DC Haynes, his young face so full of hope and eagerness. He reminded Williams of himself when he first joined the force, full of the blissful arrogance that, as detectives, they would be admired by all, solving every case with ease and being back home in time for tea. He had been so unprepared for when the shit got real on the job. The heartbreak that takes its toll, the resolve in knowing when a cause is lost and you then have to be the messenger, delivering the bad news and becoming the blame for someone's whole life crashing around them.

"Yes, inform her briefly of the situation at hand and get Mrs Payne down here as soon as possible, hopefully she can offer up some insight on her sister that could help." DS Williams instructed, already immersed once more in the stack of case notes in front of him.

"Should we get Mrs Payne's husband pulled in for interview too, if he's available?" Offered DC Haynes, eager to please.

"Yeah, why not, see if he's available to come along for the ride too. The more we can learn about Miss Carter's personality from those around her, the better hope we can have of this all having some kind of positive outcome."

"Has anyone managed to track down the landlord yet?" Williams added after seeing a post-it note on his paperwork about it. "Find out what kind of tenants the girls are, are they up to date with rent? Any complaints from neighbours? That sort of thing, we're missing something somewhere and we are rapidly running out of time!"

"We did get some information about the landlord, but we still don't have a name or a contact number. Sarah Willis said that her father signed off the lease on her behalf, so she never met the landlord personally, though she was under the impression that he owned the whole building, so we are looking to go knocking on the other residents' doors, see if they can be more helpful on that front." Informed DC Haynes.

"Ok good, the neighbour who rang in the original attack on Miss Willis, speak with him first, then get knocking door to door on all the other residents, that shouldn't take long, find out what security measures are in place." DS Williams instructed, "Though I doubt there's many, seeing how this investigation is shaping up so far." He added with an impatient tone. "Find out where everyone was last night, what they heard, when they heard it. If they've been aware of anyone loitering around recently. Someone in this village knows something and I am already running out of time and patience. So, get them door knocking now," He barked loudly, glancing at the awaiting officers in the nearby communal office, "Get calling the sister and I want as many interviews booked in today as physically possible. We need to be a bit harder with them round here or we're never going to get this case solved." With that, DS Williams turned on his heel and marched out the office, not caring to wait for a response.

Sensing the urgency and relishing his current position of responsibility working this case, DC Haynes took the reins and began delegating roles to the officers hovering around him. He was keen to impress DS Williams and wanted no stone left unturned. Splitting the waiting officers into pairs, he instructed interviews to be arranged, any necessary search warrants to be fast tracked, research and background history to be analysed with fine toothed combs and finally Kat's sister to be contacted. This could be the case that cemented his position as a permanent member of the team, with possibilities of promotions and bigger cases ahead, and DC Haynes wasn't about to let the opportunity slip away easily.

Chapter Seven

Saturday Late Morning - Yesterday

Hanging up the phone with shaking hands, Hannah could barely process what she had just been told. She knew Kat had got herself in some situations over the years but the thought of anyone intentionally harming her in any way made Hannah's blood run cold. Hannah caught her reflection in the hallway mirror, the hair elastic in her thinning dark mane, pulled up in an immaculate ponytail, suddenly felt irritatingly tight, the neat studs delicately marking her ears, now seeming pointless and distracting. She needed to be sensible with this, there had to be an explanation. Hannah had taken care of Kat from a young age and, though life and circumstance had taken them on separate paths recently, her little sister needed her again now. Hannah needed to let her husband know and they needed to pack a bag and get to Smith Cove immediately.

After leaving Ethan a hurried voicemail to get home quick so they could help find Kat, Hannah hastily grabbed her weekender bag and began collecting up things she and Ethan would need for the next few days. She had always been the organised one, she hadn't had much of a choice, but it was working in her favour at this moment in time. Quickly finding a couple of changes of clothes each, their toiletry bags, phone chargers, the essentials they would need. Hannah fumbled searching for a recent photo of Kat, one she could show to strangers in the hope they might have seen her. Hannah and Kat hadn't seen each other for a couple of years now, but surely Kat hadn't changed that much. Sorting through her photos and seeing the ones of a younger Kat took Hannah straight back to all the times in their youth when she had to be the parent instead of the sister. She never minded being there to look after Kat, and just hoped she would be there in time again. Sitting down briefly on the edge of her bed, with tears in the corners of her eyes, Hannah allowed her thoughts to drift back over the hard times, wishing she could reminisce in person with Kat.

'I Still remember doing your hair on the morning of mum's funeral,' Hannah recalled to herself, 'Pulling it back in a loose flowing plait and tying it off with the brightest orange bow. Mums favourite colour. We laughed together as we reminisced about all the funny, silly memories mum had made sure we shared. Even when she was having all her treatments and you could see in her face how it was taking its toll, even then she would make us laugh, pulling funny faces while trying on all her flamboyant head scarves as we ate waffles and jelly for breakfast. I remember clear as day her perfect, bubbly voice, full of love, telling us with a smile, "Who decided jelly couldn't be for breakfast anyway, from now on we start each day eating whatever makes us happy, that's the new rule!"

'We were only young when we lost her, you hadn't long started high school and I wasn't much older. Everyone thought we wouldn't be able to handle it, seeing mum like that in her casket. Nobody thought about how much we had already faced, watching her struggle and fight the awful disease for two full years leading up to her death, while dad buried his head in the sand and spent more and more time drinking and pretending nothing was happening. Seeing her laying so peaceful and pain free was, in so many ways, such a beautiful sight. You and I held hands for hours that day, as we smiled, cried, laughed and hugged. Heartbroken to be saying goodbye forever to our beautiful, loving mother before we had barely even reached our teens, but so relieved to never have to see her in such pain again, from the cancer or from him. We held hands as we got in the car, as we travelled home and as we walked slowly back into our house, just a shelter now, no longer a home. I remember then that you squeezed my hand so tightly that I thought you might never let go. I knew from then on it was my job to protect you, to teach you and keep you safe. Looking back, I wonder if your change in tension as you gripped my hand tighter on the approach to the house was in anticipation to the hard years ahead you knew we would now be facing, with no mother and an abusive drunk as a father, or maybe you saw Dad's sadness turning to anger as he marched on inside, already heading to the kitchen to open another bottle of whisky, and was preparing for the awful evening ahead. Holding on tight, we would get though it together.' Hannah wiped the tears from her cheeks as the vivid memories she had tried so hard to shut away until now came pouring back.

'As the years past, we grew up and grew even closer. I taught you to do your make up and how to curl your hair. I remember the time we sneaked a packet of cigarettes from Dad's desk. He was drunk again and by this point didn't know his days from the weeks, let alone what was hidden away in what drawers, so he never noticed. We tried our first cigarette together, laughing as we both coughed so much, we were nearly sick. When you first got seriously interested in boys, I was there to give you the safe sex chat that mum would have done. When one of us had a date, the other would always wait up, with Ben and Jerry's cookie dough waiting in the freezer, ready for a night of date dissection, as we laughed through all the details of the bad dates and swooned though the good ones, we had no secrets and shared everything. The last time we did that was after one of my dates with Ethan, I had been seeing him a few months and I had told you every detail of him, from the way he furrowed his brow when he was reading the financial times on a Saturday morning, to how he and his roommate had made a small fortune recently, investing in everything from new technology to property. You hadn't met him yet, but I knew you would love him too. I was so excited to get home to tell you all about the date.

"Kat, I'm home, where are you?" I sang, skipping through the front door. "I need to tell you about what Ethan said, he is absolutely dreamy, you grab the cookie dough, I'll grab two spoons!"

We sat up for hours that night as I told you the details of my perfect date, how Ethan had asked me to move in with him as we sat eating our dessert. He was just finishing university and was planning on buying a gorgeous two bed house he had found about two hundred miles away that he wanted me to move in and how I had excitedly agreed to go. It blew my mind that he wasn't much older than me but could afford it, I didn't really understand how he made that kind of money, only that he was something to do with finance and investments. I relished the fates lining up for me finally and was just so excited for my new start.

"What the hell?!" you laughed, "I haven't even met the guy yet and he's stealing you nearly, what, three? four hours away? May as well be the other side of the world! When are you planning on abandoning your sad, lonely little sister then to move in with this mysterious stud?" You asked with a mock frown before beaming me the biggest smile of support.

We didn't mention me moving anymore that evening, but we spoke of anything and everything else, talking until the sun started to come up. We talked about things we hadn't mentioned in years, silly memories we had long almost forgotten, serious moments we had soldiered through together. Knowing we would always be there for each other. When we finished chatting it felt bittersweet, we were growing up and though we would always be there when we needed each other, it was the end of something too and we both could feel it.

When dad died of liver failure a couple of years later it made sense for you to move out of the run-down house full of old ghosts and childhood memories. We set to work the gruelling task of selling the home we had grown up in and when it finally sold, you came to stay with us for the night to celebrate. You and Ethan had seen one another briefly here and there but still hadn't really met fully enough to get to know him properly and I was so relieved when he took to you like a house on fire, I just knew he would. You didn't seem to warm to him as quickly though, which was disappointing, but I put it down to all the stress that we were under with the house and losing dad. My two favourite people in the world getting on meant everything to me and I was sure he would win you round eventually.

Hannah's train of thought was interrupted with the sound of her husband hastily letting himself in the front door.

"My darling, I'm so sorry to hear of Kat, have you packed everything we might need already? We need to get there straight away and see how we can help." Ethan said, wrapping his arms protectively around his wife.

Gathering up the weekender bag and their coats, Ethan took Hannah by the hand and lead her to the car, before pulling away towards what awaited them in Smith Cove.

Chapter Eight

Saturday Early Afternoon - Yesterday

Trying to figure out my next step, I paused for a moment, contemplating pouring myself another whisky. I resisted, it was far too early in the day still for one, let alone a second and a clear head was needed if I was to continue keeping one step ahead of the game. Those officers had called me in for questioning, it was inevitable, and I had been ready for it. I'm sure they're just hoping for someone to help them out with a lead rather than them actually having any inkling of what's actually going on, but I need to keep a level head if I want to avoid jumping across into actual suspect territory. The older guy might have a bit more insight but the younger one is following the typical pattern, he's in way over his head with this case and he knows it.

I did worry at first about what Sarah would remember, I was sure she had seen my face just before I knocked her down, but the shock of it all, mixed with the Etorphine I gave her straight after she hit the floor must have distorted her memory just enough to keep me in the clear.

I hadn't wanted to use the Etorphine on Kat as well though, at least not yet, but she had been so resistant that it was the only way to keep her silent for long enough to get her out. Luckily, I knew the building layout well and I had been observing the other residents in the block long enough to know they were all creatures of habit, either out till the early hours getting wasted in the pub, or junkies locked away all the time, wasting their days trapped in their own self-made prisons, chasing their next high. To some they would seem the worst collection of tenants, but in my mind, they were the ideal residents right now, too consumed in their own miserable existences to acknowledge the goings on of those around them.

I unlocked the door and gently opened it to check on Kat, still unconscious but breathing. I have some pain relief ready for when she does wake, she's going to need it for that leg, I've wrapped a makeshift splint around it for her, but I doubt it will do much good, the damage is done. I took off her shoes too, it was the only way I could think to make her a little more comfortable, especially with the chain now bound round her ankle. If I take care of her now, she will see that I had to do what I did to look after her, the more she tries to fight back, the harder and more painful it will all be. I don't have a choice. I only want what's best for her, and what is best for Kat is doing as she's told. I hope it doesn't take too much manipulation before she realises that I don't want to hurt her any further than I already have but I have a plan, a job to do and I'm determined to see it though, no matter what it takes. Bones can mend and Etorphine effects aren't lasting, she will be fine in the long run, and once she accepts what's happening and I know I can trust her then I can tell her the reason for it all. She will be pissed, but maybe if she sees that I wish it wasn't happening just as much as she does then she might still see the good in me, I'm not an evil man, but lessons need learning and sometimes violence is the only way to teach them.

It won't be pretty for her, but people have survived worse, or at least similar, I've seen it! And she's tough, I know she will get through it, the girls before had all been weak and vulnerable, helpless without their crowd and cheering crew giving them false confidence. Not Kat, she's different. She's made of tougher things, she's delicate but she has a fearless edge to her which will give her the strength to get through this, and I will do as much I can to help her through it if she will just let me.

Chapter Nine

Saturday Afternoon - Yesterday

Looking less than her usual, immaculate self, wearing a velour tracksuit, her thick locks scrunched up in a messy bun, and no make up on her face, Sarah walked in the pub. On spotting a dishevelled looking Kane, leaning in his usual spot at the bar, talking in hushed tones with Alex, she headed over.

Sarah had been escorted home from hospital and taken into her apartment to grab a change of clothes but instructed she wouldn't be able to enter again until told it was clear to do so, which would probably still be a few hours off.

She hadn't given a second thought about needing to arrange someone to open her shop in her absence, she wouldn't miss the money, her dad would cover that for her, and focusing on Kat was more important anyway, plus her head was still feeling pretty fuzzy, in spite of her pretending to the doctors that she was fine. Kane had taken the day off from his office too, though judging by the look of him, he hadn't ventured far from this bar since last night. It seemed almost inconsiderate for the pub to be open, but the boss had called Alex first thing this morning and insisted he and Jas open as normal, saying it was an ideal opportunity to bring in extra trade. He wasn't wrong, every table had been occupied pretty much since they opened. Everyone wanting to hear more of what happened to Kat and Sarah, sharing their own theories, each more elaborate than the last. Or reporters from neighbouring towns, looking for titbits to print. Facts weren't important, the gossip and whispers grabbing momentum as the hours ticked by would be enough to satisfy their cravings, as long as the papers sold. Kat wasn't a person to them, she was just today's headline, they will have moved on to something new before the weeks out.

Seeing Sarah walk in, brought a much-needed spark back to Alex's face, though the anguish in his eyes still apparent, the relief shown with his smile. "Sarah, honey, I'm so relieved to see you up and about! How are you feeling?" asked Alex, full of concern as he headed out from behind the bar to hug her.

"I'm fine, honestly, nothing more than a bit of bruising, but I'm just so annoyed about it all. I heard it was a circus in here last night with the coppers all questioning, what a nightmare. It doesn't look much better in here today." Sarah replied, taking a glance around the busy pub.

"Have you been back to your flat yet?" Asked Kane, also gently embracing her.

"A copper just escorted me in to grab a change of clothes but for now the cordons are still there. Hopefully I can get back in there later today, I've not seen my phone since last night and the nurse said I didn't have it on me when I arrived at the hospital, hopefully it's in the flat somewhere, I mean, what if Kat's been trying to call me? God this is all just awful, isn't it? Our poor Kat, I just can't wait until she's back home and safe again."

Kane looked away, he had always been a realist and deep down he thought any hope of them seeing Kat again was wavering more by the minute, but Sarah seemed quite matter of fact that she would turn up safe and sound, and he couldn't be the one to ruin that illusion. Instead, he sat, still wearing his suit from the day before, and tried to rearrange his face to mirror Sarah's determined optimism.

"Aren't you scared though? That man was in your home! In your bedroom! Honestly Sarah, I don't know how that isn't terrifying you!" Demanded Alex, tired eyes suddenly wide with a mixture of urgency and horror.

"What are you talking about, of course I'm scared, terrified in fact that he could come back, but more than that, I'm majorly pissed off! You think I'm going to let some power hungry; dickhead scare me out of my own home? And after the bastard's taken Kat too, honestly, I wish I knew where she was so I could go help her, but I know a hundred percent that Kat will be giving him hell wherever she is. Whoever that guy is, he picked the wrong victim in our girl, Kat is hard as nails and scared of nothing, she will have that arsehole begging for mercy! Just you wait, she will be home before we know it and once she is, and she tells us exactly what's happened then that guy will be begging for the coppers to lock him up, just to keep him safe."

Hearing the heavy door to the pub open with a groan, Sarah, Kane and Alex all turned to see a far too chipper, if slightly hungover, Jack strolling through, seemingly without a care in the world.

"Where were you last night then Jack?" Interrogated Sarah accusingly on seeing him entering the pub. "I thought you and Kat were meant to be all good but then a couple of nights ago she said you've been giving her the cold shoulder for a while now. What the hell? You and I both know she tried calling you Thursday night and I'm sure I saw you skulking at the corner when I came in here that evening too, so whatever you're hiding, you best cut the crap and start telling the truth."

"Oh, back of Detective Sarah!" Spat Jasmine, appearing behind her before Jack could respond, "You've been out the hospital two minutes and you're already back in here making a scene. Why don't you nip your conspiracy theories in the bud now and get back to doing what you're best at, living with your head in the clouds, getting stoned and spending your daddy's money! If Jack was genuinely a person of interest, then the police would have called him straight in for questioning, wouldn't they? And obviously they haven't, so until they do, why don't you just keep your spiteful gossiping to yourself!"

The sudden outburst behind the bar from Jasmine taking everyone by surprise. She always seemed too wrapped up in herself to even register what everyone else had going on, let alone care enough to get involved and argue about it. Sarah indignantly turned back to where Jack had been standing to hear what his response was, but he had slipped away and was now over the other side of the pub, talking into his phone, looking a little pale and somewhat less than his usual confident self.

"Shit!" he exclaimed a little too loudly to nobody in particular when he ended the call. Jasmine was suddenly lurking nearby, keen to find out what had got him even more agitated. "That was that detective who was in here yesterday, DC Carter." He told her bitterly, "I've been called in for immediate questioning, I'm sure you'll be pleased to know!" He announced louder, looking Sarah straight in the eyes, before necking his second drink in as many minutes and storming out the pub doors.

"Well? Are you happy now?" Jas shouted, marching back over towards Sarah, Kane and Alex. "I bet you're all loving this, aren't you? Jack's done nothing wrong, it's not his fault that Kat's got herself in to whatever trouble this is! If you're all that concerned, then why aren't you out actually looking for her instead of sitting here throwing out stupid accusations?"

"Bloody hell Jas, dial it down a notch" Alex said irritably, trying to keep his cool while notably frustrated. "We would go look for her but seeing as, quite clearly, the police are involved and, quite obviously, we wouldn't know the first place to look, our most sensible and helpful option right now is to just stay put here." His patience wearing thin at how complacent Jas was acting towards them and to the whole situation. It was clear she was never a huge fan of Kat, but Kat was still in danger somewhere and Jas's attitude and mouth were going to get her in trouble soon too. "Why are you jumping to defend Jack so hard anyway, let's be honest, he's not exactly the most stand-up guy round here at the best of times, is he?"

There was a glimmer of something that quickly flickered across Jas's face, like she was contemplating something in her mind, before a smug smirk slowly spread across the sharp features of her face. "I'm defending him because I know he wasn't involved in Kat's drama, and if you want to know how I know, it's because he was in bed with me at the time the stupid cow went missing!"

The bitter satisfaction evident as Jas turned to leave, lasting just a second before feeling the sharp sting of Sarah's palm whip across her cheek.

Chapter Ten

Saturday Afternoon - Yesterday

"DS Williams?" A pretty, curly haired officer whose name always escaped his memory, called from his office doorway, "I have Jack Stanford here for you Sir. Would you like me to set him up in the interview room?"

"Ah, Mr Stanford," he mused to himself, looking through the information files in front of him before landing on Jack's. "The boyfriend. Let's see what he has to say then. Yes please, set him up in interview room two, Haynes is currently interviewing another possible suspect in one. Is there anything else we know about him yet? Background? Employment? I swear every file I have here from anyone in that deadbeat village is more clouded and vaguer than the one before it!"

"No Sir, nothing has come up yet, though we are looking in to as many angles as possible to get some stone set character profiles available." She said eagerly while tucking a stray dark curl back behind her ear, she had only been stationed in their office for the past few weeks and was keen to put in the extra leg work to impress.

DS Williams looked momentarily frustrated but said no more, before slowly exhaling while gathering up Jack Stanford's file and standing from his office chair, signalling the end of the conversation with the officer in the doorway, who then turned to leave.

"Oh, DC Watson," Williams suddenly called her back, finally recalling her name, "Could you gather everything we've found out so far about Miss Carter's last known movements, I'd like to do a fresh review of it all, in case we've been skipping something obvious, also, there's a sister listed here, a Mrs Hannah Payne, I know DC Haynes was getting in contact with her, can you chase up his team to get her interview time allocated and booked in the system please?"

Walking into interview room two, DS Williams already had a vision in his mind of what Jack Stanford would be like; cocky, arrogant, unlikeable, the kind of person who always gave a not-to-subtle impression that interviews like this were nothing but an inconvenience to them and a giant waste of time, more often than not going out of their way to play games and spew constant contradictions. As he looked up and saw Jack sitting back, looking smug and relaxed in the surroundings, Williams knew his preconception had been spot on.

"Ah, Mr Stanford, thank you for coming down, I am DS Williams, the head detective on the case of the abduction of Miss Carter. Now, obviously you are not here being accused or charged, you are here voluntarily and are, therefore, free to leave at any point, though any information you can offer us could greatly increase our chances of finding Katherine Carter sooner, so we appreciate your assistance and cooperation in the matter."

Jack, already looking bored and uninterested, stretched him right arm out to shake DS Williams' hand, though he made no attempt to stand for the introduction.

"No worries Officer, happy to help, of course." Jack responded, his voice dripping with sarcasm, "Though I'm not really sure what I can tell you about Kat that will help here. Unless a detailed description of the tattoo on her upper thigh would be of assistance to you?" He added, with a smirk.

"That won't be necessary." Williams replied, already growing impatient and inwardly disliking the man in front of him even more. "If you could tell me about the relationship between you and Miss Carter, any specific places you know of that may be significant to her, any details of the last conversations you had with her. Even the smallest of things could help hugely."

"I've been hooking up with Kat on and off for a while now. We met one evening in the pub. I had gone in with some mates for a quick after work pint and she was on shift behind the bar. She was flirty and cute, so I figured why not take her out. We've been out a few times but mostly we just hang out there or at the girls' flat. That's become a bit of a routine, once they shut the pub up for the night, a bunch of us head over the road to their place and just all carry on the evening there. To be honest I think she took the whole me and her thing all a bit more serious than I did. I mean she's not a bad girl and we did have a laugh together but I'm not really the settle down type, you know?" He added, giving DS Williams a knowing wink, which went ignored.

"Anyway, so yeah, erm, I did talk to her a couple of nights back, only on the phone though like I haven't actually seen her in a few days, but I called to let her know I wouldn't be about this weekend. She did get annoyed and wanted to talk about it but I was busy and things were all a bit crazy with me and I just wasn't in the mood to get in to it all with her."

"I had nothing to do with this though," Jack continued after realising DS Williams wasn't planning on interrupting his monologue, "I mean honestly, she's a great kid, I definitely wouldn't want to see her hurt and I don't know anyone who would. She gets on with everyone, you know, even that weird lad who's always sat there on his own. She literally talks to everyone. It's just all a bit awkward because I was actually with Jas the night Sarah was attacked and Kat went missing, and when I heard about Kat…like I said, Kat took us being together more serious than I did and we never agreed we wouldn't see other people. I've been trying to cool things off with Kat for a little while now, but it's hard to end something that's never really fully been a thing in the first place, especially when you know you're constantly going to be bumping into each other, it's not as easy as just calling it a day and cutting ties, both going your separate ways. I have been a bit quiet with her and it probably has seemed like I've had something to hide, but it's definitely not what it looks like! I honestly didn't want to upset Kat, and obviously me seeing Jas isn't really something Kat would be particularly stoked about if she found out, you know? I've not seen Kat in days, and I certainly didn't hurt her. I'm sure this is all looking like a bigger deal than it actually is. Are you sure she didn't just storm out? I heard there were traces of her blood found, maybe she just accidentally cut her hand on something as she left? Maybe somehow, she had found out about me and Jas, kicked off, and you know, just smashed the vase in a temper before storming out. We all know Kat's got a bit of a temper sometimes and she does love to be theatrical."

Knowing the interview was going nowhere, and with his professionalism being tested and patience wearing thin, DS Williams decided to cut his losses on this particular avenue of questioning for now and call it a day on the interview. He didn't really think the boyfriend was involved but he was definitely not a fan of the police and clearly wasn't interested in helping them do their job, so DS Williams didn't want to waste anymore of the time they didn't have on someone that wouldn't be adding beneficial information to the case.

"How did it go Sir, any luck?" DC Haynes questioned upon seeing DS Williams re-entering the office.

"Not really. The boyfriend was exactly as I expected him to be, arrogant and unhelpful. Though we need to call the other bar girl in for questioning. Jas? Jasmine? Have a look though the files and see what we have on her, it seems she's been messing around with the boyfriend when Katherine wasn't looking. Bloody town, more drama than it's worth going on round there!" He said, sounding exasperated. "How did you get on with your interview?"

"Yeah, much the same, not very productive. He seemed helpful enough, but he didn't have much information that we didn't already know. He said he tends to just go to the pub for a change of scenery and wasn't much of a talker. He did say that as he lives in the flat above Miss Carter, if we need any further info then to just call him back in and he will be available."

"Shame they can't all be that willing to help, I feel like we're chasing our own tails with this case at the minute."

Chapter Eleven

Saturday Afternoon - Yesterday

Sitting, restless in the passenger side of the car, Hannah watched impatiently as Ethan slowly filled the tank with petrol before meandering over to the kiosk at a painstaking pace. Ethan would never use pay at pump, instead opting for a slower paced, human interaction inside, even if that meant queuing for what seemed an eternity. This never normally bothered Hannah too much, she found it a little frustrating sometimes and it had caused a minor bicker between them on occasion but today she found herself increasingly infuriated with his gentile demeanour.

Everyone always tells her how lucky she is to have Ethan, how she had landed on her feet, but the truth was that when they met, Hannah had been wearing rose tinted glasses, she wanted a prince to whisk her away from her awful excuse of a father and carry her into the sunset to start a new, better life. It wasn't until she got everything she had hoped for, that she realised the grass wasn't always greener. Ethan turned from a gentleman to a dictator over night, he provided her with the security she so desperately craved but at a cost. Kat had reservations about him from the start, she always got on so well with everyone, but even after the very first time she and Ethan met, Hannah could tell Kat was wary of him. Hannah never asked why, she was too afraid of Kat's honesty, bursting her bubble of her new life. Hannah had been so keen for them to get on though, the two most important people in her life getting on would make everything fall in to place for Hannah. That was why she had insisted on Kat coming to stay for a night or two after they sold the old house. Maybe that's why it all went wrong, perhaps she had put so much pressure on this new, perfectly balanced life, that it was doomed to fail. Hannah had never had a fairy tale life so maybe she was just kidding herself when she thought it could be happy families and happily ever after for them all. Since that weekend Ethan had encouraged Hannah to branch away from her troublesome sister, he had seen how hurt Hannah was, that rather than staying over and spending some real time together as planned, Kat had instead upped and left during the night with some feebly transparent excuse about having urgently been called in to work. Ethan had insisted

Hannah would be much happier finding a friend or two locally or a hobby she could immerse herself with rather than causing herself unending stress dealing with her little sister's daily troubles. Hannah tried focusing more on herself and on her new relationship status with Ethan but as for local friends, Ethan was so critical about who she spoke to and persistent about her befriending just the girlfriends and wives of his selected friends, that Hannah ended up becoming more reclusive, opting to spend the majority of her free time alone. It was peaceful, lacking any drama, just how she liked it. The lifestyle suited her, life moved on and she became distracted from Kat. As it was, Hannah hadn't spoken to Kat in a couple of years now. Hannah guilt tripped herself often about it, but convinced herself it was for the best, Kat seemed independent and thriving on being a free spirit, whereas after years of having to grow up too fast and be responsible, Hannah felt that being taken care of financially and having stability and security was exactly what she needed, even if it increasingly made her feel trapped these days.

"So, what's the agenda for when we get there?" questioned Ethan, climbing back in the driver's seat, handing Hannah a pre-packed ham and cheese sandwich and a bottle of water. "Eat that please, I doubt you've eaten anything yet today."

Hannah took the sandwich obligingly but opted against opening it, instead just taking a sip of water.

"I've got to check in to the police station to speak to the officer heading the search for Kat, then after that I'd really like to track down and meet her roommate, I can't believe what the police said they've both been through, I just can't shake the feeling that I've let Kat down, I should have been there, been more hands on to help look out for her and keep her out of trouble."

"Sweetheart, you can't blame yourself, Kat is more than old enough to look after herself now, you can't be held accountable every time she makes foolish choices, you looked out for her long enough." Ethan remarked. "Besides, even if you had wanted to, how would you even have got hold of her, I thought you said her number was no longer in service when you last tried?"

Hannah looked away, finding the guilt hard to shift. She still hadn't forgiven herself for letting Ethan talk her in to not inviting Kat to their wedding, he convinced her that

Kat wouldn't come anyway and if she did then she would have caused drama and ruined Hannah's day. Ethan caught her and let out a sigh.

"Look," he said, his voice softening, "You know I care for Kat, she's your sister which makes her a part of my family too, but we both know she has always had a habit of finding trouble, this is exactly why I was so glad when you stopped going on about her, just the thought of her turns you in to a worried mess sometimes, imagine if she hadn't of cut you out and you ended up visiting her in that dumping ground of a village. Kat loves you in her own messed up way, I'm sure, but she wouldn't hesitate to drag you in to the same messes she keeps finding herself in."

Hannah knew there was some truth in Ethan's words, Kat had always been a beacon for trouble, it wasn't that she sought it out, more like she had some magnetic force that pulled chaos towards her. Hannah had lost count of the number of times over the years that she had ended up intervening to prevent situations getting worse for Kat. She had never minded, sometimes in fact even relishing in the excitement of the anarchy surrounding her little sister, but since adjusting to a more peaceful life with Ethan, Hannah had felt the pressure of control and responsibility ease from her shoulders. The relief of an easier life making Hannah put blinkers on when it came to her sister. Adopting an 'if I can't see or hear of any drama around Kat then I'm sure it's not happening' outlook. Now the blinkers were well and truly off, and Hannah felt full of dread at how much her sister needed her when she hadn't been there.

Chapter Twelve

Saturday Evening - Yesterday

Waking up, feeling groggy and disoriented, Kat willed her eyes to adjust to the darkness surrounding her, eager to figure out where she was and how she could get herself out of this mess. Trying to pull herself up to a more stable position she felt an excruciating pain stabbing through her left leg. She knew instantly it was broken, the pain already unbearable. Her arms felt heavy, like she had slept awkwardly on them or had them held up for too long. Feeling a fresh wave of panic flood through her, Kat tried to keep herself calm, desperate to piece together the distorted flashes of memory she had from the past few hours. Was it only hours? Days? Minutes? However long she had been here, she had no idea.

Focusing all her concentration on blotting out the physical pain firing through her body and the panic and fear swirling in her mind, Kat felt her eyes slowly bringing the minimal surroundings encircling her into vision, thanks to the barely worthwhile side light in a far corner which had been turned on for her. Nothing helped in pinpointing where she was, but there was a plastic water bottle and a paper plate with some dry cereal and an apple on it. Had someone just brought them in for her? She could see the faint outline of a single door. She couldn't see any windows, it was too dark, but there was a slight breeze coming from somewhere. Trying to be as calm and logical as she could, Kat brought her focus on to herself. She could feel that she was still wearing her jeans, but her boots and socks were missing. She couldn't see the colour but guessed from the feel that she still had the grey tee shirt on she had been wearing. The thought of her still being clothed was strangely reassuring in spite of the ominous situation she was currently in.

She could see a figure in her hazy memory. Was it a man? What about him could she remember? Growing frustrated at herself with the feeling she was missing something obvious and important from her memory, she grabbed the water bottle and drank thirstily from it.

"Hello?" Kat croakily called from the darkness. "Whose there? Why are you doing this to me?" Her voice holding together, making her appear less scared than she really was. "Please, I don't know what you want from me but I'm in a lot of pain, please just let me go."

Kat could feel the swelling on her cheek, and the side of her head felt tender and bruised. She vaguely recalled being thrown to the ground and hitting her head. Was that into this room? How did she even get here? She wondered to herself, impatiently willing more clear information to hit her hazy memory.

She had been in her flat, she could remember that much. She had just got home from running errands all day, but something was wrong. Think Kat, think! Where was Sarah? Kat recalled seeing Sarah's Gucci boots she always wore everywhere standing neatly by the wall and her chunky, light brown handbag hanging by its strap over the side of a chair as she walked through the door. But why couldn't she remember actually seeing Sarah? Pleading with her memory to provide her with the missing pieces, Kat remembered someone else coming out of Sarah's room, making her jump. She recalled a feeling of surprise and panic, before the man struck her across her face. Willing the memories to keep returning, Kat remembered touching her hand to her nose then and feeling warm, sticky blood pouring from it. The fog in her mind slowly clearing more and more now as she remembered reaching out to grab something to defend herself with. The vase on the side table. Kat reached for it and felt her blood-stained fingertips brush the edge, but the man grabbed her hair and whipped her back, causing the vase to smash to the floor.

Sitting there now, Kat could see it all like a camera lens coming slowly in to focus. The man forcing something over her mouth. A shirt or a cloth of some kind. She recalled how she felt suddenly drowsy and drunk. The next thing she remembered was being thrown to the ground. She still had no memory of what had happened to her leg but right now that was the least of her worries. She could hear someone close by, unlocking the door separating them from her, and just as the fog cleared and Kat finally remembered the face of the man who had attacked her, he walked in, confirming what she already knew.

Chapter Thirteen

Saturday Evening - Yesterday

Taking a mouthful of his long forgotten, now barely lukewarm coffee, DS Williams sighed to himself, not for the first time that day. It had been a strenuous few hours, full of tiring interviews that hadn't seemed to help at all in getting them any closer to putting the case to bed. Rubbing his eyes roughly with the palms of his hands, he stood from his note covered desk and stretched his back. It was nearing twenty-four hours now since Sarah's attack had been called in, so the only time scale they had for Kat being taken was then too. The fact that there was evidence of Kat having been abducted by the time Sarah was found, mixed with the fact nobody had interacted with Kat all day yesterday, left a very broad window of time that Kat had been missing for. Best case scenario they were working with twenty-four hours, worst cast would be around thirty-two hours by now. DS Williams dreaded the thought of how this would end, from his own past experience, anything over thirty-six hours was usually a devastating result with nothing but bad news as closure for the searching parties.

He had two more interviews to get through before the evening was out, DC Haynes had interviewed Kat's sister, Hannah Payne, as soon as she checked by this afternoon, but there had been no officers free to speak to her husband, Ethan Payne, at that point. He had been eager to help though, offering to go out searching for Kat and to come back to the station later in the evening when somebody was free, so DS Williams had agreed to squeeze him in personally for an interview. The last interview of the day was one of the other staff members from the pub, Mr Alex Milton. DS Williams wasn't holding out much hope that either interview would be a great deal of benefit but maybe one of them would point them towards something that was so far amiss, and both Mr Payne and Mr Milton seemed much more willing to cooperate and help than some of the other interviews that had been held so far that day.

"Mr Ethan Payne has just arrived for you Sir." DC Watson informed him, swapping out DS Williams forgotten coffee with yet another fresh one. "Front desk has signed him in and he's now waiting in interview room two. I'm clocking out now, DC Smith and DC Andrews have just arrived if you need anything." DC Watson dithered momentarily in case DS Williams required any further assistance from her, before equating that he was already once more consumed with the notes scattered in front of him. "Goodnight, Sir." She added, half-heartedly as she left.

For a second or two DS Williams resented how DC Watson and the others could just clock out and switch off back to their own lives, but this is what he had signed up for. Over the years he had drifted away from his wife and children, always being more focused on his work, until eventually his wife divorced him, taking their two daughters and moved away. He barely noticed at the time, always so distracted by the case in front of him, too committed to the job to split his attention with much else. Lately though he spent more and more time wondering what he would have done differently if he could, often wondering to himself what his wife and daughters were doing now and whether they were safe and happy.

He didn't know what to expect of Ethan Payne, but DS Williams had always based a lot on first impressions and instincts. Walking into the interview room to see him sat there, smart suit, neatly cut hair, already preparing to stand to introduce himself, DS Williams found himself giving an appreciative flicker of hope, Ethan Payne seemed a world away from the time wasters and troublemakers he had interviewed so far. The fact he wasn't a local was evident from the start and Williams was more than grateful for it.

"Thank you so much for coming in Mr Payne." DS Williams announced his arrival with an outstretched hand.

Ethan stood, brushing down the front of his suit jacket and returned the handshake with matched enthusiasm.

"Not a problem at all, I'm more than happy to help, the sooner this is all sorted and Kat is found, the sooner we can all settle and get back to our lives."

"I completely agree, this is a case none of us want lingering and I will do whatever I can to get everything resolved in the fastest time possible. If you could give us any insight into Katherine Carter, any personal history or anything you think could assist in our search, any small details could make all the difference."

"Of course, and I am very happy to help, I know my wife certainly won't settle until she knows what's happened to her sister, though I do worry that Kat's nearest and dearest round here may well have given you a somewhat rose-tinted view of what Kat is truly like. Of course, I can only give my own opinion, but from previous personal experience, Kat invites trouble. She's pleasant and bubbly and instantly likeable, but unfortunately you need an honest and unbiased character profile of Kat, if you're going to have a fighting chance of figuring out what's happening here. My darling wife, Hannah, would be furious at me for telling a truer account of her sister, but we all have the same aim here, and that is, of course, to get my little sister-in-law found safe and sound and away from trouble as soon as possible. With that in mind I'd like to paint you a more realistic picture of Kat that you may have so far. She's a great one at playing the nice girl act, being all friendly and flirty, but as soon as someone reacts to it, if you know what I mean, she suddenly flips the play and starts acting all innocent. Girls like that are always going to come unstuck sooner or later. I'm not trying to suggest anything sinister here, but maybe she just played the tease with the wrong guy at some point, and it all got a bit carried away."

"In fact," Ethan went on enthusiastically, "Is anyone absolutely certain that she has actually been kidnapped? Since I first met Kat, she has always been a little flaky, jumping from one fantasy to the next, I really wouldn't be surprised if she had met a guy somewhere and disappeared with him for a few days on a whim and just forgot to charge her phone. She's more than likely having the time of her life somewhere, completely oblivious to all the worry she's caused back here. It wouldn't be the first time Kat's done something similar, last time Kat came to visit with my wife and myself, she suddenly upped and left in the middle of the night. No note, no explanation."

"While I'm very grateful for a fresh perspective, and we would love the outcome of all this to be just a matter of Miss Carter having gone on an unannounced adventure, I'm afraid that wouldn't explain Katherine's blood on the broken vase at her property or why her roommate had also been attacked. I would very much like for your theory to be correct, Mr Payne, it would certainly make my job here a hell of a lot easier, but the fact is that all evidence is pointing at Miss Carter being removed from her residence against her will, with no sign of her since, therefore we must assume she is still being kept against her will, the important question we're all eager to answer though is where?"

"I understand." Ethan replied, sounding somewhat deflated, "Though I'm still certain this is just a misunderstanding and Kat will turn up soon, absolutely fine. Please just let me know how I can help in the meantime. I have money, if I can fund any appeals for her, put up a reward for information, anything like that, I'm eager to be involved, if I could just ask in return that you keep me updated with any developments, obviously I'd like to be there for my wife if she is going to be receiving any bad news."

"Of course, I completely understand, I'm sure this is all a lot for your wife to process. Thank you for coming down Mr Payne, please do get in touch if you hear anything or if you think of anything at all that could help. My extension number is on the card here." DS Williams stood, handing Ethan his card and stretching out his hand to shake Ethan's, drawing the interview to a close.

Chapter Fourteen

Saturday Night - Twenty-Four Hours Ago

I couldn't believe it when she moved in to that flat, I was already keeping an eye on her, watching as she flitted from one friends' sofa to the next, she had never even registered me, but when she moved into that exact flat, it was more than a stroke of luck, it was fate. I had kept track of her from a distance for a while, making a hundred percent sure it was her, biding my time and playing the long game, then, when I knew I was tracking the right girl, it was just a matter of time. She was exactly how I pictured her, every inch of her so approachable, it would be easy to gain her trust, I had a job to do, and I would get it done. Over the last few weeks though, getting closer and closer to her, it had been impossible not to start to care for her. She seemed so vulnerable up close, I just wanted to look after her, teach her to be stronger, I couldn't prevent the grudge that had brought me here, but I could help her fight back, or I could find a way to look after her myself and keep her safe. I fantasised about changing the narrative and becoming her knight in shining armour, I could save the day and whisk her away. Away from him. Away from everyone here. A brand-new life, just me and her, I would love her with everything I had, and all she would have to do is accept it and learn to love me in return.

It had gone too deep now though, all the strings being pulled were no longer in my control, I had a job to do and it was as simple as that, time and energy had been invested, there was no way I could back out now, it wasn't in my nature to back out on a deal, besides which, I'd just end up gaining a target on my own back too, but maybe I could manipulate the situation a little, just enough to keep her safe and out of the direct firing line, while still remaining loyal. She had done wrong in the past and upset the wrong person, and she had to pay for that, it wasn't up for debate, but if she listened to me and worked with me rather than trying so desperately to get herself away, then it would all be so much easier for everyone involved. I am losing patience with her stubbornness and reluctance to do as she's told, if this is how she was acting before then it's no wonder she got herself in this trouble in the first place. Watching her now, I wish I could explain to her why I was doing this. In time I will, but for now I need to stick to the plan and not allow myself to become distracted because of my own infatuation. I don't want to hurt her, I want to love her, and if breaking a couple of bones now keeps her scared enough to listen and stop trying to disobey me, then it will be worth it in the end. I will apologize until she knows I have nothing but love for her, but right now I'm as trapped in all of this as she is. I'm getting paranoid, I thought I saw him earlier heading into the pub, I followed to see for sure, but I couldn't spot him in there anywhere.

After placing the tray of food and painkillers down beside her sleeping, angelic, though somewhat bruised, face, I slowly tiptoed out and locked the door, just as the phone in my pocket begins to buzz.

"Hello?" I answer reluctantly.

"I need an update! What's happening with her? Is she scared yet? Conniving little bitch, I can't wait to see her suffer, she thought she could embarrass me like that and just walk away? Let's see how smug she is when I'm done with her."

"I've got her here, I think I need more time though, she's scared but I think I can push her further, really have her panicking." I say, trying to buy her and me both some more time.

"Fine, you've got twenty-four hours and I'll be there to take her off your hands. After that you can consider your debt paid for good. Great work buddy."

I know what he's planning to do to her, and the thought makes me sick. He had always been one to get his own way, especially with women, whether they were interested or not, even back in college, once he set his sights on a girl then he would make sure he got her, regardless of whether she returned his enthusiasm. Early on when we met, he caught me hacking the college computer system, I was good with technology and business, a combination that if you were smart, could make you a fortune as long as you didn't get caught. I was good at it and was already making fair money. I reluctantly offered to bring him in on a deal, get a few cheats and investments behind us both if he just kept quiet. He agreed but added his own terms to the deal, that I just had to keep some girls quiet from time to time. It seemed like a vague, stupid term, so I agreed, not really knowing what it was I was agreeing to. The first time he brought a drunk girl back to our dorm room I wasn't needed; I hadn't registered how quiet she was until the next morning when he bragged to me about how easy it had been to drug her so he could take full advantage. I was so disgusted in him, but he told me how she had been flirting with him all night, pretending to be interested and playing him just so she could take advantage and get him to keep buying her drinks. Using her looks and leading him on just to drain his wallet and arrogantly expecting to give nothing in return. She was nothing but a fucking tease. Girls like that are a different breed, entitled and think they can just take guys like us for a ride. They use us for their own benefit then toss us aside. I no longer felt disgusted at him, she deserved it, taking advantage of him all night, he was just levelling out the playing field and taking advantage of her right back. Over our college years this happened a few times more, I ended up enjoying the satisfaction of knowing we finally had the upper hand. I got stronger and smarter, knowing exactly how to manipulate each girl before he took over and did his part. I'd always turned a blind eye when he took over, kept well out the way and just done my part, convincing myself that those girls deserved everything they got. But not Kat. I can't have him hurt her like the others. Once we left college and went our separate ways, it was a few months before I heard from him again. We had been making good money with investments and he said he wanted us to get a property set up in Smith Cove. He told me there was a girl who had been a tease to him, just like before, and we needed to teach her a lesson like old times. I was hesitant and he knew it, but he assured me that after this last time he would call us even on any secrets and we would part ways for good, investments and all.

Twenty-four hours. That's it, if I pull this off and keep him happy while keeping Kat safe then twenty-four hours from now I could have everything I've always wanted, I'll be free from his clutches, I'll have all the investment money and I could have Kat all to myself forever more. I just have to figure out how to balance on the wire, keeping him satisfied that I did all I could, while showing Kat that, in spite of what I've done to get her here, I only want to keep her safe. Going round in circles in my head I finally had the solution. If I let her go then he would one hundred percent know I'd gone against him and let him down, he would never forgive me and I'd forever be looking over my shoulder, just waiting for him to punish me, but if I took photos to prove to him I'd got her here, showing the chain restricting her, her broken leg and the bruises on her face, that way he would know I was loyal to him. Then, if she managed to escape on her own, that would be out of my control, she could go missing for good as far as he was concerned, but this time she would be safe with me. He would never know. I just have to find a way to let her escape without her knowing I'm helping her.

Chapter Fifteen

Saturday Night - Twenty-Two Hours Ago

Feeling restless and exhausted and like they were facing nothing but goose chases and dead ends, DS Williams took a long pull on his cigarette. He had given up several times over the last few years, convincing himself that each last one would be the true last one, but every rough case seemed to bring him straight back here, the fresh box of Mayfair in his desk drawer, only purchased that morning, now already almost empty. Something had to give with this case, what the hell was he missing? He was growing increasingly frustrated with himself. A couple of hours ago they had started re-interviewing anyone they thought might have something beneficial for them, knowing the sand in the hourglass was trickling away quicker than they hoped and they were edging nearer to it running out for good. He took one final drag before stubbing the cigarette out on the wall and heading back inside. Checking his notes as he walked through the over-lit corridor to the interview room awaiting him.

"Mr Heath, thank you for coming back in, especially at this time of night and on such short notice too. I am DS Williams, I know you were previously interviewed by DC Haynes and your cooperation was greatly appreciated, however, some fresh information has come to light, so we are working through second interviews as effectively as we can. My apologies if you therefore find the process repetitive. If you could just give me a brief summary of your relationship with Katherine Carter, when you last saw her, any information you may know from living in her block of flats too. Go ahead Mr Heath."

Already looking somewhat crestfallen, Lucas let out a sigh, his shoulders dropping low, like he had the whole weight of the world resting on them. "I know what everyone round here thinks of me, I hear them chatting all the time. When you're quiet and sitting alone people almost forget that you can still hear them, or maybe they just don't care if you overhear. Saying petty playground comments, 'Lucas, he's such a weirdo, he's so quiet, why does Kat even talk to him.' I know that everyone's going to be pointing the finger at me, but honestly, I care for Kat more than anyone, I would be lost without her and the only reason I'm here right now is to do whatever I can to help find her."

"I assure you Mr Heath, nobody here is accusing you of anything, you are not here as a suspect, just as someone who can hopefully help us towards solving this case and bringing this whole ordeal to a close sooner rather than later. Could you tell me a bit about your own relationship with Miss Carter?"

"Kat and I have been friends for a while now, we talk about everything. She is the only one round here who even gave me a chance when I first started finding my feet and venturing out in the village. Yes, I'm quiet and awkward sometimes and I know I don't really fit in, but when I first spoke to Kat, she made me feel confident. I was heading to the pub one evening to try and get to know the surroundings, but I must have got there late into the night. A small crowd had started to gather outside while someone was locking the door. Kat saw me standing there awkwardly, I must have looked disappointed or lonely because she smiled at me and invited me to tag along with the crowd. I wasn't too sure, but everyone was smoking and chatting and laughing and then the whole lot just went across the street towards my block of flats and I kind of just got herded along too figuring I would head back home. We all ended up in a little flat on the floor below mine though, I went in with the rest of the crowd and found myself standing alone, wondering what I was even doing there. Torn between finding the confidence to go and attempt to make conversation with my neighbours or just turning around, heading out the door and climbing the stairs to my own, quiet home.

"But while I stood there, she came over. Kat. Not looking confused or pissed that I, a complete stranger, had actually joined the gathering in her home, but friendly, laughing. She asked me about myself, and I don't know why but after a while I found myself opening up to her, telling her things I'd never told anyone, things I was ashamed for and had tried to keep so firmly locked up in the abyss. Suddenly it all just spilled out from me. I told her I had recently moved in above her and that I was nervous to meet people. I told her that I was trying to escape my past and was keen for a new start here. I even told her about my stepdad, how he beat me black and blue every week for five years when I was a kid, before I finally ran away and lived on the streets. I moved around a lot, trying to keep safe and desperate to find a way to salvage my life somehow. I told Kat about the woman who had taken pity on me and offered me a gardening job in exchange for cash and food, but then started wanting other services too. I told her how I hated myself for it, but I had no other option and I just kept thinking of the end goal of getting myself straightened out and that awful part of my life being a distant memory. I worked my arse off, saving every penny until I could afford to put myself through college. When I finally had enough cash, I packed my scruffy backpack, jumped a train and headed towards my new life. I enrolled in college, got myself straightened out, even started making myself some real good money. Then recently I got assigned a new job, which led me to this little village. I told her all this and yet she still wanted to talk to me." Lucas turned his face away from DS Williams, tears that we're briefly evident in the corners of his eyes instantly wiped away.

"I care about Kat more than I have cared about anyone my entire life. She is the kindest person you'll ever meet, checking up on me, keeping me sane. The thought of anyone wanting to hurt her is outrageous. She is always so kind to everyone, so happy and friendly, I'll do anything to keep her safe." He continued, his previously emotion filled face full of expression now becoming an almost emotionless mask.

"When I last saw her briefly in the hall outside her flat on Thursday, she seemed different. Not upset but distracted. She told me she had just had another argument with her boyfriend and was thinking of going to stay with her sister for a few days. That was all she really said before we said goodbye and I headed up the stairs to my own flat. It was only a few minutes after I got in my front door, I was about to jump in the shower when I heard her screaming. I got dressed so quick and ran down them stairs so fast I almost fell, I thought maybe Kat and her boyfriend had got in another argument and he had hurt her. When I got there the door was open, I could see the pooling water and the chunks of broken glass on the floor from the vase that must have been knocked over. I went in and saw Kat's bag on the sofa but no sign of Kat or anyone else. When I checked the bedroom, that's when I found Sarah unconscious on the floor and rang you.

"I didn't see anyone else in or around the flat and I honestly have no clue who it could have been, but maybe her boyfriend would be the best person to be investigating.

If there's anything I can do to help then of course I will, but I really don't know anything more, I just hope she is safe and stays that way."

Chapter Sixteen

Sunday Early Morning - Twelve Hours Ago

Hannah busied herself around the dive that was their current room in Smith Cove's only bed and breakfast. It was dingy and appeared not to have been cleaned since long before their arrival. She knew though that even if it had been a five-star hotel with the plushest bed available, she still wouldn't have slept any better. Hannah had waited for Ethan to come back after his interview at the station, but he had text and said he was going for a much-needed drink and suggested she got an early night and caught up on a bit of sleep. Early in their relationship she would have offered to join him for a drink or two, so he could talk through what was weighing him down, but these days she knew better, when he said he was going for a drink, Hannah knew that was his way of telling her he wanted to be alone, so she stayed back in the stale room, feeling agitated and restless, worried for Kat and frustrated that she didn't know how she could help her sister in her time of need. Hannah didn't want an early night, her mind was too wired, at some point though she must have drifted off on the chair, as when she woke at around five the next morning, Ethan had returned and was snoring, still fully clothed on the bed.

Having a quick shower to wake herself fully, Hannah allowed her mind to wonder back to previous memories with Kat, wondering to herself how they suddenly got here. With Kat in trouble and missing and Hannah not knowing anything about her current life or what trouble she's facing.

"We had always been thick as thieves growing up." Hannah thought to herself. "There wasn't anything we wouldn't do for each other. In recent years though things had changed. We hadn't had a falling out, but the connection between us had altered on that last time we saw each other, it was tense and forced, not like how it used to be. It was when I had finally convinced you to come stay for a weekend and meet Ethan properly. I had high hopes of you and me sitting up half the night chatting and laughing like we used to, and of you and Ethan getting on instantly. First introductions had gone well, and everything seemed relaxed, but before the evening was out you told me that you had a feeling about Ethan and you thought I should cut my losses and get out while I still could, before things got too complicated. I knew you hadn't been happy about how I had moved so far away with someone you hadn't even met, so I took it on the chin and let it go, with just a slight feeling of deflation. After that strange moment though, you seemed ok and Ethan was being nothing but charming around you, I saw you laughing and relaxing, so I figured whatever your issue had been, you were over it just as quick. You had always been like that, everything was a seesaw, dramatic and serious one minute, and then switching back to happy and easy-going the next. I had learnt to love it about you.

The following morning, you were gone before I was even awake, I called you, telling you to come back for breakfast at least, but you refused, insisting something had come up at work and that you had to rush back. You turned all serious again, you made me promise to call anytime at all that I needed you, and to remember what you said. I didn't take it seriously though, Ethan was one of the best things to ever happen to me, I figured you were just jealous, making dramatic scenarios up in your head and lashing out about Ethan purely because you were used to being the most important person in my life and weren't keen to now share the role. You had no need to be jealous or insecure though, you were always so important to me and that was never going to change, whether we spoke regularly still or not."

Sitting there now, Hannah kicked herself for not reaching out to resolve things sooner with Kat. They had spoken on the phone every once in a while, and Kat had told her a few milestones, like when she started working in the pub, but the calls were kept short and the text messages blunt, the closeness the pair once shared had faded and been replaced with a wall of reservation between them. Hannah had grown up and moved on to a calm and settled life with Ethan, and Kat had returned to her carefree lifestyle, not feeling the need to check in all the time. The were both happy so the applecart remained un-rocked for a while. Then when Hannah, in spite of Ethan's objections, had tried to call Kat before the wedding, she found Kat's number was no longer available.

Heading out of the shower and hastily brushing her teeth, Hannah peered round to see if Ethan had roused at all. He was still snoring away and if the stench of alcohol on him was anything to go by, Hannah figured he would stay in his pre hangover land of nod for the foreseeable future. She quickly dressed, grabbed her bag and left without looking back. Finding Kat was the only reason she was here, and she had no time to wait around just to play nurse to his self-inflicted fuzzy head.

It was almost seven in the morning now but, like Ethan, the sun had yet to rise. Hannah walked nervously through the harsh glares from the streetlights, willing them not to disappear before the daylight started to break. The heavy downpour of rain from the previous night had eased, transitioning into a constant drizzle, the type that didn't seem heavy enough to worry about at first but left you damp and cold to the bone within minutes. Pulling her Parka tighter around her chin, Hannah searched around for a café or anywhere that was open where she could warm up and think things though. She knew Kat must live near to the pub she worked in but didn't know the exact address, if she could find the pub then hopefully someone there could help Hannah get closer to figuring out what had been going on with her little sister.

After what seemed like forever and yet no time at all, Hannah found a pub she figured must be it. Hannah remembered Kat calling it, somewhat strangely, the Strangler's Arms, the run-down pub now standing in front of Hannah had a slightly wonky sign labelling it the Wrangler's Arms, so Hannah took her chances. Shielded as much out of the rain as she could, huddled under the battered awning over the side of the building, Hannah lent against the peeling paint of the window ledge waiting for someone, anyone to arrive.

Chapter Seventeen

Sunday - Today

Sitting at his usual spot at the bar, with a not too satisfying coffee in front of him, Kane looked around at the early morning drinkers nursing their pints and picking at their mediocre five piece fry ups, consisting of an under cooked bacon rasher, a blob of cold beans, a river of tomato juice stemming from the single tinned tomato, a fried egg of almost rubber like consistency and a microwave reheated sausage hot enough to burn your mouth. One or two customers having paid extra for the slice of burnt toast on the side. The Wrangler's Arms was their place in the world right now but fine dining it most certainly was not, though the punters surrounding him didn't complain. The locals had all learnt better than to expect much more and if they did ever dare complain then the chef wouldn't think twice about coming out from his microwave filled kitchen and telling them to 'fuck right off home and make it themselves then!'

He could barely remember the last time he ate and knew starving himself would be of no help in the hunt to find Kat, so reluctantly Kane weighed up his minimal options, debating whether to order a bacon sandwich and risk getting food poisoning or cower out and just grab a bag of ready salted and be done with it.

Unintentionally making the decision for him, Alex appeared with a plate of toast and two fresh coffees. "Don't panic," Alex half-heartedly smirked, "The microwave tech is out back having a fag. I nipped in quick to do your toast while he wasn't watching, less risk of it being burnt that way."

"Thanks babe." Kane replied, returning a half-hearted smile of his own. "Have you spoke to Sarah, any updates on Kat yet? I can't believe all these locals in here," He added, brandishing his arm at the punters scattered behind him, "Not even two full days ago Kat gets abducted and Sarah gets attacked in her own home and these wasters are in here, milling over their fry up and pint acting like nothings even happened and they haven't a care in the world, for fuck sake, what the hell is wrong with people?"

Kane rarely lost his cool and even less frequently swore, he was generally more reserved and tactful with his comments, the polar opposite of Alex, who had no social filter and swore constantly in conversation without even realising. Under normal circumstances Alex would have made a joke about it, how Kane was always too suave to lower himself to the level of the rest of them, but on this occasion, he just gave Kane's hand a reassuring squeeze and took a sip from his own coffee.

"Sarah was in here about an hour or so ago actually. It was all a bit crazy, when I turned up to open first thing this morning there was a girl crouched down out in the rain by the front window, I thought it was just some drunk but when she noticed me unlocking the door she stood up and raced over. She looked sober as anything, definitely hadn't been drinking and didn't seem like a junkie or anything like that, she didn't fit in round here though, seemed way too upper class for Smith Cove, but her eyes seemed desperate, and she looked bloody freezing, so I told her to come in and warm up while I got the bar ready. Turns out she's Kat's sister and was desperately trying to do whatever she could to achieve what the local police didn't seem to be doing, find Kat. I got her a coffee and something to eat and was just trying to figure out what our next step would be, when Sarah came in. I didn't even know Kat had a sister but when I introduced them, Sarah seemed to know all about her, so I left them to it. Shortly after that they left together, heading over to Sarah and Kat's flat, I've not seen or heard any updates since though."

"Jesus Christ, I had no idea Kat had a sister either, I wonder why she never mentioned her to us. What else don't we know about her?" Kane asked rhetorically, mulling it over. "Maybe this actually was a personal planned out attack then and the answer could be right in front of us, we just never asked the right questions. Hopefully Sarah can get something useful out of this mysterious sister and we can finally have something decent to cling to, because honestly Alex, I'm starting to think the worst." Kane choked out, looking away before Alex could notice the tears forming in the corners of his eyes.

Alex wasn't used to seeing Kane lose control of his emotions, whether temper or tears, he was usually so in control of himself. Deciding that the coffee just wasn't cutting it by this point, Alex grabbed two small glasses from under the bar, turned to the optics hanging behind him and poured two double whisky's, downing his there on the spot before turning back to Kane to hand his over.

"Drink this babe, I think you could do with it. I'll send Sarah another text and see what's happening over the road with her and Kat's sister."

"Thanks." Kane replied distractedly, grabbing the glass and sipping it slowly, allowing the heat from the whisky to travel through him while the smooth liquid caused a not-unpleasant burn in the back of his throat.

As the pub door opened, the familiar sound of sirens could be heard travelling on the screaming late autumn wind outside, causing Alex to give an involuntary shiver where he stood. Sirens were as common a sound as the ticking of a clock around Smith Cove, but now the sound was hitting different, each wail of a siren mimicking their internal wails of desperation for finding Kat, intensifying with their own panic, growing louder and more suffocating with every passing minute.

Kane And Alex's day was spent between long silences, strong coffees with whisky chasers, feverishly typing out and sending unanswered text messages, and trying and failing to come up with ideas of how they could help. Finishing his last whisky in the early evening Kane began to stand from his stool while grabbing his Parka.

"We've waited all day, I can't wait anymore, I'm going over to Sarah's, I need to know if she's found out anything that will help..." Before he could finish his sentence, the wailing of sirens and screeching of tires on the rain-soaked road intensified as several police cars pulled up facing the flats opposite, causing everyone in the pub to turn and stare through the grubby stained windows as they all fell silent.

Chapter Eighteen

Sunday - Today

Walking across the road to the flat together, Hannah instantly felt at ease around Sarah, it was like she had always known her. For the first time in the past twenty-four hours, Hannah felt a fresh sense of optimism in their search for Kat, assuring herself that between the two of them, she and Sarah could figure out something that so far everyone else had managed to miss. From what Hannah had learned, Smith Cove was a rough area, with crime and disturbance everywhere. Though while petty thefts, rows and cheap drugs seemed to be the norm, kidnapping and the unthinkable crimes that could go along with it were, thankfully, less of a regular occurrence. So, what had made Kat the victim of kidnap? Ethan had insisted Hannah not get involved with playing detective, suggesting that if anything she would just cause more confusion so she would be better off trusting the police to do their job and handle the situation properly, but once Hannah spoke face to face to Sarah, and saw her own worry and frustration mirrored in Sarah's face, she knew they couldn't just sit by and hope any longer, they needed to step up for Kat and do whatever they could to help find her.

As her foot crossed the threshold into the flat, Hannah felt the instant presence of her sister surround her, the invisible embrace of Kat's persona and spirit encompassing her making Hannah feel like a teenager again, when all she and Kat really had was each other. The connection they had was stronger than most, they were sisters, yes, but they were also best friends for a time, and each other's only safe space after the loss of their mother. That connection had faded and stretched over the years but being in Kat's flat now, Hannah felt an overwhelming urge to protect Kat once again, she could feel Kat's lingering presence embracing her, the sensation making Hannah feel like she could almost reach out and feel Kat by her side, willing her sister to appear safe and sound next to her. The awful situation was making Hannah realise how much of her own self she had abandoned when she and Kat had drifted apart, she had become downtrodden and wary of her own shadow. She had a sudden realisation that since Kat had stopped contact, slowly but surely more and more of Hannah had faded along with her. Hannah's decisions, what she cooked, what she wore, where she went, even where she worked, had been made for her by Ethan. She had become a controlled, silenced Stepford wife and almost completely lost her protective, strong, determined sense of self that their mother had embedded in to her two daughters. That was changing as of right now. Kat needed Hannah and Hannah was here, she needed to look after her little sister and figure this all out, and then she would hold herself high and make some much needed changes in her own life too.

Sitting down together, Hannah and Sarah tried to figure out the first of so many unanswered questions that faced them. Was Kat a random victim of circumstance, an unplanned target for a dangerous chancers attack, or was something more sinister lurking, had Sarah been the one in the wrong place at the wrong time getting attacked, just like the police told her, whereas Kat had always been the intended prize victim for an evil monster with a more personal incentive.

"Let's think this through." Hannah spoke out loud, taking a sip from the tea Sarah had made. "Whoever it was who attacked you and took my sister must have got in here somehow, without breaking the door."

"That's what been bugging me so much about all this," Sarah replied enthusiastically, "Me and Kat both only had one key each. Kat had lost hers at Jack's. He's an absolute dick but it wasn't him, he was too busy boning that stuck up bar bitch the night Kat was taken." Sarah added with a fresh wave of anger on Kat's behalf. "The guy who attacked me came out of my room, but I wonder if he thought it was Kat's room instead. My window wasn't open, and neither was Kat's, the coppers confirmed that, so whoever he was, he must have come in the front door. It couldn't have been tampered with because it unlocked fine with my key when I came in that evening, so what are we missing here?"

Hannah and Sarah both sat in silence for a few minutes, drinking their tea without really tasting it, too focussed on the unanswered question facing them.

"Wait," Hannah suddenly had a thought, "What about your landlord, surely he has a key?"

"Yeah, I guess he must do," Sarah replied, not really sure of Hannah's train of thought, "I've never even met him though, I couldn't even tell you his name, I just know he owns this whole building and doesn't live round this way."

"How do you get hold of him if there's a problem?" Hannah persisted.

"It's all managed through some agency; I remember when I moved in my dad had been asking the guy on the other end of the phone a lot of questions. He said something about the landlord and how it was a guy who bought the whole building over the phone before it had even finished being built, he had never even visited for a look around before putting in a full asking price offer and was renting all the flats out on long lease only, something about him not wanting loads of quick changeovers of contracts. Apparently, he came down once, for a security check or something like that, just before they went on the market to rent, but then he signed all the management responsibilities over to a private agency and hasn't been down since, as far as I know none of the other residents have ever met him either.

"Do the agency have a key?" Hannah pressed on. She didn't know what she was hoping to find out, but she felt strongly this was the avenue to get the answers she so desperately craved.

"I really have no idea." Sarah responded absently. "Hang on, let me see if I can find the number for them and I'll see what they say."

While Sarah went rustling through an array of previously discarded paperwork, looking for the agency's details, Hannah tried to pull any relevant information she could from her memory about owners and agents. Ethan had been buying, selling and renting out property since before she had met him, He started small while still in college and hit a couple of good investments and escalated from there. She never got involved in his business, but she did recall him sometimes working alongside other investors and agencies. It was a small chance but maybe he might know of someone from the agency who could help, he has so many contacts in the business.

Trying, and failing, to get hold of Ethan by calling, Hannah remembered the unconscious, drunk state she had left Ethan in, before rolling her eyes to the heavens and frustratingly typing out a message instead.

Call me. ASAP. I need to get hold of Kat's landlord

and don't know where to start! I just have a feeling this could lead us to Kat. Do you have any contacts round here Ethan? Can you help? x

Hannah figured Ethan was either still snoring away on the cusp of waking up with a hangover or was now awake but full of self-pity and probably didn't even know where his phone was. He always became somewhat withdrawn and defensive when something was wrong or he had a lot on his mind and often turned to drinking, more often than not alone, Hannah didn't usually get too annoyed about it and just tended to stay out of his way for a day or two while he got whatever it was out of his system, but this time it was bothering her a lot. He was meant to be here to support her and to help find Kat, but he seemed so distracted before his interview, insisted on going to the station alone, saying he needed to clear his head on the way there.

Sarah came back to the sofa with an array of crumpled up paperwork, there was more than enough to sort through, and it wasn't filled with much useful information, but it was a start, Hannah could look over it and hopefully somewhere amongst it all would be a phone number or email address or something at least linked to the landlord that she could try, while Sarah continued searching the flat.

Hannah was eager to follow up this new possible lead, she wasn't holding out too much hope, but it was a new avenue for them to try and any information they could get from just making a couple of phone calls would be a step forward for them.

What seemed like an eternity, though was probably only a few short hours, the streetlight outside coming on, indicating the early November sun was already preparing to set, after searching through all the paperwork scattered around the flat, hidden in drawers, pinned to the fridge, stuffed into bags, Sarah finally found the contract from when she moved in. Skimming through the agreement papers Sarah had just past her, Hannah instantly felt an odd sensation of familiarity, something about the paperwork felt like deja vu, she recognised something she couldn't quite place within the officially worded document, like a distant memory from another life, and as she spotted the details printed at the very bottom of the last sheet, Hannah's blood ran suddenly icy cold within her veins.

Chapter Nineteen

Sunday - Today

Pacing the room, unable to relax, I checked my phone for the call I knew was coming. I had spotted him walking around, so it was only a matter of time, he hadn't yet seen me, but it didn't matter, he knew I was there, and the inevitable phone call would be coming any point now. I had played my part, somewhat reluctantly by this stage, but I had done what was asked of me, I held up my side of the deal and did what I had to do. I had followed the plan we had spent months meticulously plotting out and aside from a couple of inconvenient snags, we had stayed on track to the end game. We had done similar plays in the past, maybe not this intense but they followed the same pattern, so why did this one feel so different, so much more personal?

I knew the answer. It's because it was personal this time. It wasn't just some random girl on a night out that had shunned him or pissed him off. It was Kat. Precious, genuine, beautiful Kat. I hadn't planned to get attached, but there was just something about her, even after I befriended her and gained her trust, knowing what would happen to her now, I always hoped I could do something to save her from her fate, knowing, deep down it had always been out of my control. I had a job to do, and I had got it done, if I had of refused or intervened then it wouldn't have mattered, he would have killed me and still found a way to go after her. That was the power he had always held.

The phone next to me buzzed. The phone call I had simultaneously been eagerly anticipating, so this could all be finished with and anxiously dreading, knowing the cruel next step it would hold, finally coming.

It wasn't a long chat. They never were. Just a calm, emotionless update and instructions to meet.

"I'm sure Kat's sister knows. Meet me in one hour, I'll text you an address." With that, the phone line cut out, back to silence.

I had to keep my focus and stay calm, this was just a job, once it was done, I could forget the whole thing and move on, just a few more hours and it would all be over.

I could feel the stress building inside of me as I made my way to the train station. I wasn't going far and wouldn't be gone long, but I was suddenly keen to leave the village, even just for a short time, to regain control of the situation and my nerves. The dank village of Smith Cove had become an invisible noose slowly tightening around my throat, making every breath slightly more difficult to take than the one before it.

Every step I took further away from Smith Cove, I felt the tension in my muscles easing and the feeling of calm washing over me, I needed to stop looking at Kat as someone I cared for and had wronged, when in fact she had upset him, she was the one who had wronged him and until she paid for that and accepted her punishment, balance wouldn't be restored. This is what I needed, a bit of breathing space to gain clarity back over the situation, the constant battle inside my own head now temporarily calms once more. He would tell me the steps now that needed to be done and then my role would be over, debt repaid, and slate cleaned.

***

It had been a more detailed meeting than planned. He spoke like it was any other business transaction and reminded me that was all it was too. He had always managed to help me regain focus and see the big picture. Returning back on the train I felt ready, it was like old times, we were in control and Kat was just getting taught a lesson she wouldn't forget for her behaviour in the past, she would learn from it and not make the same mistakes again. We could draw a line under the whole thing and finally we could all move on from this nightmare. The late autumn air bitter and sharp as I stepped off the train platform, shocking my senses to life. The rain filled clouds above creating a darkened blanket, suffocating all of the village beneath it. I could feel the adrenalin pulsing through me now like electricity, this was my comfort, blending into the darkness.

As I made my way home, passing through the shadows, I remembered being told how quickly you adjust to the shift in atmosphere after the night creeps into the village. The constant wailing of the sirens, tearing their way through the streets. The screeching of tires as the late-night workers, keen to get home, crossed routes with the boy racers, torturing their remodelled bangers in a vain attempted to make them the fastest. The all-night music blasting from the dishevelled student housing block on the corner, where it appeared to be one continual rave. It was true, I had become immune to it, walking alone was no longer something I dreaded, making me feel vulnerable and weak in a darkening whirlwind of lights, sounds and chaos, instead I found myself savouring the lonely, late-night journey, finding the night-time chorus almost a comfort now.

What was putting me on edge tonight was the noticeable absence of the usual evening soundtrack. No sirens, no screeching tires, no thumping base pounding from the corner house. The deafening silence creating a menacing feel, as though any moment a lurking monster would appear from behind the eerie shadows and rip my little world apart.

I quickened my pace and found myself looking rapidly around, searching for the source causing the burning feeling that I was being watched. The echoing of my footsteps appearing louder each step and almost out of time with my own. Were they just my footsteps echoing? I couldn't be a hundred percent certain with myself now.

The ominous sense of someone or something watching me from behind the shadows, mixed with the noticeable lack of the normal night-time village sounds was messing with my head. Something didn't feel right. The sudden roar of an engine as a car appearing from nowhere sped past me, causing the cat laying on the road to give a shrill wail as it jumped up, darting across in front of me, only to be instantly engulfed in a darkened alleyway a few metres down from my side. The paranoia setting in making me almost run now. I couldn't put my finger on it but something was definitely off balance tonight and I needed to get home so I could breathe again. It was probably just my overactive imagination. In the usual busy sounds of commotion from the streets around me, I felt invisible, blending into the night, as though whatever I did or wherever I went wouldn't be noticed, just how I liked it. But in this eerie silence I felt vulnerable and seen, painfully aware that my world could unravel in the blink of an eye if only someone chose to pay the slightest bit of attention to me. Then they would all know the truth. The reality that the real monster walking these streets and turning the village upside down was me. I needed to embrace the role I had taken, there was no space for error or reservations now. Over the past few years, I had done a lot of bad things and turned a blind eye to the unthinkable. Kat may have thought she had suffered at my hand but now he was finally here, it was about to get much worse. I need to get back now, get back to Kat. This is it, my last chance. To do what though? What could I do? Warn her? Help her escape? I can't. Deep down I know she will never forgive me for everything that's happened, even if I was to help her get away. All that would do it put me at risk from him too. I desperately want her to be safe from all this, but at what cost? Can I afford to risk losing everything, risk losing my life, just to protect someone who will probably never want to be near me again anyway? But what if she did? Maybe she could feel about me the way I feel about her? If I managed to get her away from him before it got worse, then maybe she could build feelings for me? I could finally have everything, or was I about to lose it all?

I can't listen to all these different voices in my mind anymore, walking in this eerie evening silence, with nothing but the cruel sound of the bitter, wailing wind is messing with my head. I just need to get back.

Chapter Twenty

Sunday - Today

"What is it?" Sarah nervously asked when she saw the colour drain from Hannah's face before her.

"The firm at the bottom of this letter..." Hannah hesitantly replied, willing the information in front of her eyes not to be true, while knowing in her heart that it was suddenly clear as day. "P&H Property. That was one of Ethan's earlier company names. When he was at university and first delving into investments, he made a company with a friend, Somebody Heath. The P&H stood for Payne and Heath. I asked a couple of times who this Heath was, but Ethan just shut me down, saying business was just that, business, and I had no need to get involved. Then shortly after that he finished university and moved on to a new company, so Heath was never mentioned again, and I never gave the name a second thought."

"But if that's true, then your husband owns our fucking building!" Sarah blurted in horror. "And Heath, why does that name ring a bell?" She added, mind whirring in overdrive at the shocking information Hannah just unloaded on her.

Almost hysterical now, Sarah grabbed her phone and passed Hannah hers too. "I'm so sorry Hannah, I can't imagine how you're feeling about all this, I'm sure Ethan is a decent guy and this is all an utterly awful coincidence, and I'm sure he has a good reason for not getting back to you already today, but you need to get hold of him right now, please keep ringing him, I'm going to phone the police while you do, and we just need to hope upon everything that this lead finally connects us back to Kat."

***

"DS Williams, sorry to interrupt but I have a phone message for you from Sarah Willis, Katherine Carter's flatmate." The pretty, dark haired officer whose name had once more slipped Williams' memory announced into the room. "She said that she and Katherine's sister…" The reporting officer paused to double check the notes she wrote just minutes before in front of her, "…Hannah Payne, have found some important information regarding ownership of the building that they think will be of urgent interest to you."

Putting down the crumbled notes he had been reviewing for the umpteenth time today, DS Williams took the message from the officer and carefully began reading through it.

"Jesus Christ." He announced to nobody in particular when he had finished reading. "Get a car to bring in Ethan Payne for questioning straight away! It all seems a bit too much of a coincidence that he is linked to that building and linked to Katherine Carter and yet chose not to mention it, even to his own wife!" DS Williams instructed the female officer. "DC Haynes, read this and see where we're at now, then get a unit out to find and detain Lucas Heath, the upstairs neighbour, as soon as physically possible, I have a strong feeling he is the 'Heath' from 'Payne and Heath', and I think we may have missed something detrimental during our previous searches. Get a team over to Heath's flat right now, I want it searched from top to bottom." The urgency in his voice contagious as everyone in the office began making calls, alerting units and heading out the doors. They were about to find something now, good or bad DS Williams couldn't predict, though his gut was leaning towards the latter, but something was about to come to light.

Chapter Twenty-One

Sunday - Today

How long she had been there, Kat had no idea by this point. There was something vaguely familiar about where she was, but the exhaustion and panic had numbed her thought process. She was becoming delusional, convinced that she had heard her sisters voice calling for her in the darkness, minutes or days ago. The concept of time in the bleak darkened surroundings was lost to Kat, the only indication of night or day was when a smidgen of light taunted her through the pin prick sized hole, she had no way of reaching. It was impossible of course, that she could have heard her sister here, as far as Kat could tell, the only way in or out of her prison space was through that door. And even if someone could reach Kat, she regretfully imagined Hannah would be the last person to come looking for her. Allowing her thoughts to drift back to when she last visited her sister and how Ethan had ruined the girls bond forever in the space of just a few hours, Kat felt a silent tear slowly descend down her cheek, wishing more than anything that things had been different.

The visit to Hannah and Ethan's new place had been fine at first, Kat had been oblivious to how her drinks had been flowing faster than she would have intended. Ethan had been playing the dutiful host and topping up Kat's glass regularly whenever it dropped below half full, making it impossible to keep track of how many she had drank. It was Kat's first time properly meeting Ethan and he appeared just as Hannah had described him, mature, smartly dressed, charming, though a little too brooding and authoritative for Kat's liking and there was something off about him that Kat couldn't quite put her finger on. Seeing her sister with sparkling eyes and a permanent smile though made Kat give him the benefit of the doubt. Kat couldn't recall when she had last seen Hannah so happy and relaxed, probably not since before they lost their mum all those years ago. The girls were having the best time catching up, just like old times, careful though to only be recollecting the positive moments of their earlier years together. The dark cloud that hung over the decade or so following their preteen years was something both girls had always silently agreed never to mention, adopting the childlike mentality that if it was never spoke of then the awful moments during those times never really happened, almost like a scary dream. They shared memories of their mum, long before the cancer took hold and before he started becoming abusing and relying on the drink from morning till nightfall. Remembering family trips to the beach, playing card games on the floor in their holiday caravan, Christmases giggling as they sneaked peeks at the beautifully wrapped gifts under the tree, singing carols while their mother baked, and burnt, gingerbread in the tiny kitchen of their family home. Getting lost in time stumbling cautiously down memory lane, until at some point in the evening Hannah suddenly came over dizzy, Kat hadn't thought she had drunk so much to take that effect, especially with Hannah always being so sensible and aware of herself, but Hannah was slurring and losing her balance, so Ethan had helped her to bed. At that point Kat should have called it a night too but she had been having a tough time recently and the drinking was numbing all sorts of problems and memories she was fighting internally with, including the ones of her abusive dad, she had kept them successfully locked away for all these years, but trying not to recall those particular tales tonight had caused the opposite effect, with Kat now struggling to keep her buried nightmare of a past life from rising to the surface of her mind once more.

When Ethan returned from getting Hannah safely tucked away in bed, pouring Kat another glass before setting himself next to her on the small sofa, Kat hadn't read anything into it. He started telling Kat how Hannah had confided in him about how Kat had been bringing her down and how much happier she was since stepping away and since Ethan had become a part of her life. It hurt Kat to hear but she had always known she was a handful, draining her older sister of so much freedom and happiness. Hannah had never said as much to her, but Kat often felt like a burden to her, and she couldn't deny how content and relieved Hannah seemed in her new life. Ethan told Kat this was the perfect opportunity for them to get everything out in the open and for her to finally stop forcing Hannah to look after her and make the separation without Hannah being made to feel guilty for it. Ethan told Kat that it was something Hannah had mentioned often but that they both knew Hannah would never say it to Kat and if Kat brought it up then Hannah would deny ever feeling that way, let alone having ever mentioned it, so it would be better for everyone if Kat just left and broke away from Hannah now. The mixture of heartbreak and alcohol bringing Kat to sudden tears. Ethan placed his arm around Kat to comfort her, until he was suddenly stroking her thigh, telling her that they could still get to know each other a little more intimately before she left as he had made sure Hannah wouldn't be waking up any time soon to catch them in the act and if Kat ever tried to tell her then Hannah wouldn't believe Ethan was capable on breaking her trust anyway. Kat, not having consciously noticed that Ethan hadn't in fact been drinking the evening away too, put his sudden sleazy actions down to him maybe being drunk and getting carried away, Kat laughed nervously, brushed his hand off while standing and staggered away to the kitchen. She hadn't expected to feel the sudden force of him behind her, knocking her to the floor. Feeling a mixture of drunk from the alcohol and fuzzy from the sudden shove to the floor, Kat looked dizzily up to face her unexpected attacker. Ethan's expression now a twisted one of anger and enjoyment combined, while Kat's own expression turned to one of horror and instant recognition of the horrendous situation now facing her as she saw Ethan hastily unfastening the zip on his jeans. Knowing she couldn't face trying to recover from that kind of violence again, Kat knew she had to do whatever she could to get away right now. Using the door frame to support more force, Kat used all the energy she could muster to ram her feet into the back of Ethan's lower leg, bringing him to the floor alongside her, hitting his head as he landed. Panicking, Kat had expected Hannah to rouse and walk in at any point. She knew Ethan's earlier words about how happy Hannah was because of him and how Kat always brought her down, painful as they were to hear, had more than an element of truth to them. Kat had always relied on Hannah when things got tough, and Hannah had always stepped up to the challenge, until Ethan had rode into Hannah's life like a knight in shining armour, provided her with a safe home and a much-needed sense of calm and protection that she had always secretly craved. Kat knew Hannah still loved her and cared for her but if she walked into the situation now with Ethan unconscious, trousers undone and a drunk Kat beside him, would it be a step to far for Hannah to process? Hannah had settled into her quiet life with Ethan with a sense of relief and seemingly nothing but pure love for Ethan, and Kat could only see how the situation could be so completely misread and look like bitter revenge for Ethan stealing her sister away. Hannah wouldn't care to listen to how Ethan had been set to abuse Kat, Kat was sure she wouldn't believe it, she would only have focus for how Kat had caused Ethan physical harm out of, what, jealously? Hannah hadn't walked in though, maybe she had drunk more than Kat realised and had passed out in an alcohol fuelled slump, dead to the word until the hangover kicks in. Kat quickly checked Ethan was breathing and after being fairly confident that he was, she stood with a struggle, grabbed her bag and left for the train station without looking back.

She had a couple of voicemail messages from Hannah after that, the first was the next morning, a confused Hannah asking why Kat had left in the middle of the night but with no mention of Ethan. When Hannah rang again a few minutes later Kat had spoken to her briefly and created an unconvincing work scenario she had to return for, before ending the call. The second voicemail came a few days later, a much angrier sounding Hannah stating that Ethan had told her what had happened and that maybe it was, in fact, for the best if they all kept some distance now. Kat wondered what Ethan's version of events had sounded like and knew regretfully that any chance she had of convincing Hannah she was building her life with a monster had now since past. Anything she said now would look like bitter lies, created out of spite, and would achieve nothing more than to push Hannah further into Ethan's arms and wedge Kat out indefinitely.

Forcing her thoughts back to the present, Kat tried to calm her breathing while she hastily wiped the fresh salty tears from her face. If only she could reach that tiny corner of light she kept glimpsing, if it was disguising a window then even if she couldn't get out of it, maybe she could get someone's attention outside who could help. If only her broken leg would allow the movement. The pain in her leg was excruciating, but she knew better than to take the painkillers that kept being left for her. He pleaded with her to take them, saying how much he hated seeing her suffer more than she needed to, but seeing as he was the one who had caused all this pain, and he clearly had no intention of letting her go free, Kat feared for what the tablets actually were and how much further they could incapacitate her. Between the broken leg and the other leg chained up, Kat already was at too much of a disadvantage, adding unknown medication to the mix would just escalate the trouble she was in. He told her she needed to trust him, that he wanted to help her and agreed things had gone too far but that this had to happen and to take what pain relief he offered now before it was too late, because someone else was on their way and it was about to all get much worse. Kat wasn't sure how much worse it could get, but was determined to fight to the end, for as long as she possibly could.

Chapter Twenty-Two

Now

Hanging up the call, Sarah turned to fill Hannah in on what DC Watson, the female officer on the phone, had made of their newly discovered information. If the unexpected link to Kat's brother-in-law had taken her by surprise, she hadn't shown it through her voice. She had taken it seriously though and requested that both Sarah and Hannah stay put at Sarah flat for the time being, in case an officer comes by for further information.

Heading through to the living room, Sarah found Hannah staring blankly out the window, her eyes red and puffy and the remnants of tears leaving streak marks down her cheeks.

"Oh Hannah, I'm so sorry for everything you're having to deal with, I'm certain we can still find Kat, she's so strong and will be absolutely fine, and I'm sure it's all just an awful coincidence that your husband's old company are involved with the building, maybe he never mentioned it because maybe he genuinely never even realised. I mean if it was an old company and he bought and sold several properties, maybe he completely lost track of this one. Besides, I thought you and Kat had barely spoke in a few years, she's only been living here a few months with me, how would Ethan have ever known?"

Wiping her face roughly with her hands, Hannah turned to face Sarah before a fresh tear trailed from the corner of her eye. "I wanted to talk to Kat so many times after I last saw her, but Ethan always told me it was for the best if I didn't. He said she brought something out in me that he didn't like and that we would all be better off if she and I kept living our more separate lives. I convinced myself for a while that was true and settled on the reasoning that if she needed me then she would call. I spoke her a few times briefly but for nothing more than a generic routine update on our lives. I did finally pluck up the courage to call her again a while back, I had been thinking a lot of things over and I knew it was time to really speak to Kat and build bridges once more. I called her while Ethan was out working but the number was disconnected. I had no way of really knowing where she was living, or any way of contacting her without coming here myself, all I knew was what she had previously told me, that she was sharing a flat near the pub where she worked. When Ethan proposed I was so happy, but I knew I needed my sister there with me. When I told him that though, he completely lost his temper, I'd never seen him like that before. He began shouting and calling her awful names, saying she would drag me down in to her games and I'd end up with nothing, just like her. It was horrible, she's the only family I have, but how would I even attempt to fix things with her if Ethan wasn't on board, he never would have let me come here alone. Then on the other hand I had my husband to be, who had provided me with everything, a home, security, affection. How could I upset him over someone who had moved on, made her own life and hadn't cared enough to stay a part of mine. I didn't bring it up again. Ethan took charge of the wedding arrangements, he said he wanted it small, not a circus for the benefit of everyone else, but just a quick afternoon in the registry office, just to make it official then an evening away, just the two of us. I had no friends and no family aside from Kat, so that seemed the most sensible choice. I didn't even have a wedding dress. It was just about us officially being married, me becoming his completely. The notion seemed romantic, until our wedding night. I had a couple of glasses of champagne, why not, surely, we were celebrating, but I must have had one too many because Ethan told me I was making a fool of myself. When I mentioned Kat again, saying I wished she had seen her big sister get married, his face contorted into something sinister and ugly. He said that now we were married, things would be changing, if I wanted the housewife life, living in a nice house, wealthy husband, and security…especially security, he knew how much I craved a safe and peaceful life…that it was about time I started showing him more respect and doing more as I was told.

That night, out first night together as a married couple, when I climbed out of the shower, Ethan dragged me to the bed. Before I could even react, he was climbing on top of me, roughly kissing me, effortlessly pinning both my hands above my head with one of his, before forcing himself into me. I screamed out in pain as he thrust himself into me again and again. It was a lesson. I belonged to him now, he held all the cards, and he knew it. That was the real reason for the marriage, it was about control. After the ordeal, Ethan went and showered, leaving me silently sobbing on the bed. When he returned, he wrapped him arms around me, apologized for hurting me and said that it was just because it upset him so much that on the day that was meant to be about just me and him, I ruined it by mentioning Kat. He said I made him feel like the house, the money, the stress-free life, him, like it still wasn't enough, that all I cared about was the sister that I didn't see. He looked so hurt and genuine in that moment that I felt I deserved what happened, that I had caused it by being selfish. He was right, everything I had is what he gave me, I'd have nothing and be nothing without him.

From then on, I never mentioned Kat again. Maybe if I had been stronger and more determined than I could have found her and kept her safe." Hannah's voice waivered as a steady stream of fresh salty tears followed the tracks of those before them. "Kat warned me about him, but I didn't want to hear it. She told me not to trust him, that there was something about him that made her nervous, that reminded her of our dad, but I shot her down, convinced it was all in her head." The silent tears falling at their own will slowly down her cheeks.

Sarah didn't know what to say. Kat had told her briefly over a couple of bottles of wine one night about her sister and her overbearing husband. Kat had said he was a control freak and that something had happened that she didn't want to speak about, but Sarah had no idea just how far he was willing to go to exert that power and control.

"I don't think the coffee is cutting it." Sarah stated at last. "Kat needs us, and we are going to figure all this shit out together." She added, giving Hannah an affectionate squeeze on her arm. "You go get yourself freshened up, I'll nip across to the offy and grab a bottle of something stronger, I know that copper on the phone told us to stay put but I think you could do with it, and I know I definitely could. I'll be back in five, I promise."

Walking out through the building lobby, Sarah knocked straight into the odd guy from upstairs, Lucas, causing him to drop all the post he had just taken out of his mail caddy. Kat always told Sarah he was actually fine but there was something about him that Sarah just couldn't shake. He seemed flustered and keen to escape, rushing himself up the stairs before Sarah even said a word. Narrowing her eyebrows in frustration and distain at him, Sarah turned to leave before noticing an envelope Lucas had missed, picking it up to put back in his post tray, Sarah found her eye glancing at the name on the front. It took half a second before recognition kicked it and Sarah's eyes grew wide. Immediately abandoning her plight for the shop, and with the letter still in her hand, Sarah turned on the spot and as fast as she could, ran back to tell Hannah the awful realisation that there was just one too many coincidences happening now and that the only logical conclusion was that the Heath in 'Payne and Heath Property' was none other than Lucas Heath, the weirdo living right above them.

Chapter Twenty-Three

Now

Dragging her broken leg behind her, wincing with every painstakingly slow movement, Kat was determined to reach the single shard of light that kept breaking through to her. Her hopes were pinned on it proving an escape, a lifeline to get her out of this nightmare. The lack of food she had eaten since being locked in here, combined with a severe lack of sleep and the searing pain from her leg, the promise of hope coming from the tiny triangle of light felt miles away, rather than just two or three metres. Up until a short while ago, Kat's non-broken leg had been chained to a pipe on the wall, she guessed it to be part of the central heating, definitely not something she could break without noise and a struggle, but when he came in a little while ago to offer her some painkillers, he accidentally dropped the key for the padlock holding the heavy chain in place. Kat was sure he noticed, almost as if it was deliberate, but when he left the room, he still left it behind. She didn't know if it was a trap or not, but he had said something about 'it was about to get much worse', so she didn't have time to ponder what was coming next for her. Kat had no choice but to at least try everything she could to break herself free. Kat's eyes were getting used to the darkness enveloping her now and thanks to the faint glow coming from the little side light in the corner that had been turned on one more, she could just about make out the keys full outline against the floor. Knowing time wasn't on her side, Kat willed herself on, mustering all the small amount of strength she could find to stretch her fingertips as far as they could possibly reach, scraping the cool metal of the side of the key. Pleading with herself not to accidentally push it out of reach, Kat concentrated hard, wiggling marginally closer as much as the makeshift cuff on her ankle would allow, before taking a deep breath and trying once more, catching the key this time with the tip of one grubby fingernail. If she had enough strength to do so, Kat might have cried again, but the clock was against her, and this was her only shot. Scratching the key along the floor until she could firmly grab it in her hand, Kat fumbled several times before finally feeling the key click into place, turning it and releasing her good ankle from the cold metal shackles binding it.

With no time to let the relief set in, Kat was straight on to the next part of her escape plan. Keeping one eye and ear to the faint distinguishing outline of the door, she used her arms to drag herself closer and closer to the glimmer of hope coming from the little beacon of light shining in on her. Willing herself not to pass out from the immense pain in her broken leg and the feeling of fire pulsing around her now released leg, Kat relentlessly persevered, moving clumsily, ignoring the wail from her bones, willing her to rest. She didn't know how long she had but it was only a matter of time before he was back to check on her and then that would be it. With that in mind and having finally reached the shred of hope she had been clinging to since Lucas trapped her here, Kat pushed herself up on her one good leg. Immediate touch told Kat her instincts had been right, the cool, condensation covered glass of the triangle had to be a window, and now she was closer she could feel the sheet of all black vinyl covering it, acting as a complete blackout screen, all but the tiny space where the condensation droplets must have repelled the adhesive of the vinyl, causing it to start to peel.

The elation and hope she now felt spurred Kat on to remove as much as she could of the clingy material. She strained her eyes to try to see through the tiny little hole but all she could see was a blur of muffled light coming back to her. Not a lovely, welcoming parade of heavenly sunshine but the grey, subdued tones of a dirt covered streetlight dully glowing through the darkness of the dreary autumn sky, and yet it was the most beautiful ray of light Kat had ever seen. Muscles weak and pleading against her, she painstakingly peeling against the stretchy, sticky material keeping her hostage. Kat fought through her exhaustion until she pulled back a piece with such force it took half the imprisoning sheet with it. Raising her head to finally look out at the new surroundings and further her escape, Kat felt a fresh wave of horror flood over her. She knew this view. It wasn't quite right, the angle was different, creating a slightly different perspective but this was definitely the same view. The streetlights shone bright enough through the dark sky for her to recognise the buildings and distant shadow of the sea staring back at her. She had sat and watched the sun set over those same houses she was now facing numerous times from her very own bedroom. The angle was wrong, but it was definitely her view. That made no sense though, it was her view but not. She couldn't figure it out until suddenly it clicked into place, it was her view but a few metres to the left. Holy shit, she thought to herself, as realisation and relief sunk in. She was in the empty apartment right next to her own. Lucas lived above Kat, he would have known it was empty too, Kat wondered briefly to herself how he had managed to break in and get the locks changed so he could come and go without anyone ever noticing. The relief that all she had to do was get the attention of a passer-by, possibly even someone she knows, and she would be free, home well and truly within reach. The madness of it all, so many unanswered questions, fear suddenly feeling less weighty, and knowing she was finally just moments away from being noticed and escaping this ordeal, Kat found herself suddenly laughing at the insanity of it all. Whatever reason Lucas had to of done this to her didn't matter anymore, she would be free, and he would be a problem for the police to deal with.

The thought of being so close now building her enthusiasm to continue peeling off the window covering. Focusing all she had on the task at hand, Kat didn't hear the door unlocking at first. As it suddenly slammed from behind her, Kat felt her whole body suddenly tense up. Lucas would be there, waiting for her to turn. He did drop the key though, Kat still thought it was deliberate, so maybe, just maybe she could plead for him to let her go. Slowly turning around, Kat felt the last of the energy she had leave her, as she saw, not Lucas, but Hannah's husband, Ethan, staring down at her with the same awful look in his eye and evil smirk he had on the last time she had seen him standing over her like this.

"Oh Kat." Ethan smiled menacingly at her. "I believe we have some unfinished business." He added, before slowly undoing the zip on his jeans and dragging her by the hair with sudden force away from the window.

Chapter Twenty-Four

Now

Hearing Ethan close the door behind him, I winced to myself, knowing what Kat was in for. The girls who came before her wouldn't have remembered about Ethan. They might had felt the effects after, but they were either too intoxicated when it happened or completely knocked out from the Etorphine. He was always careful to cover his tracks, always girls he didn't know and who wouldn't know him. If they went to the police to report their unknown attacker, he had never been in trouble enough for them to have his DNA on record. He had always been smart and remained untraceable. Once he had played his cruel game and had his fun, he would leave them before they woke or sobered up. It was their own stupid faults for being such fucking teases and then allowing themselves to be so vulnerable. Girls like that needed teaching a lesson and bringing down a level or two. He just announced himself to Kat though, so however this was going to end, I couldn't see Ethan letting Kat go free without a fight first. I tried so hard to help her. I didn't want to put her in the hell she was now facing against Ethan, but I had no choice, I was backed against a wall, if I'd refused then I'd be dead by now, and when I took the job on, I had no idea I would find myself caring for Kat like I do. Ethan's always been like a brother to me, he's all I've ever really had to look up to. what was I supposed to do? I did what I could. I pleaded with her to take the painkillers for her leg, so it didn't feel worse. I felt so awful about hurting her, but she was fighting against me, and I panicked and saw red, I lost control and have hated myself for it since. I couldn't just let her go free, Ethan would have known and then what would he have done to me? But I tried to guide her to escape, I made the hole near the window, just a tiny hole in the screen, barely big enough to notice at first so it wasn't obvious I knew about it, but just enough that she would realise there was another way out for her. Then I purposely dropped the keys. I wish she had eaten more of the food I left her over the last couple of days, then she would have had more strength, but I had faith she could do it, that she would escape harm's way and it would still look to Ethan like I did everything we agreed.

It was too late now. I had done everything Ethan asked and was finally free from his debt after all these years, but in doing so I had failed Kat. All I could hope for now is that he would let her live after he was done with her, and she would recover from this. If ever she would see me again, I would explain to her that I was a victim in all this too, I had no choice and no control. Hopefully she would understand and see that I would still be so good for her. With the slate wiped clean I could look after her properly, she would want for nothing, we could move away and live happily ever after, just her and me.

Heading into the apartment I had been living in for the past few months, I acted quickly and efficiently. I didn't have many possessions here, living here had only been a cover while I tracked Kat, it was never my home and now I couldn't wait to be gone from it. We already had the contracts all signed and ready to go to unload the building ownership to a local estate agent, it had no use to us after tonight. As I started packing the few possessions I had into bags and my minimal clothes into a pull long holdall, folding each piece with intricate uniformity, desperately trying to distract my mind with the task at hand from the pain Kat was about to experience, a sudden pounding on my door sent my nerves scattering.

Feeling the walls suddenly closing in around me I hurried my bags out of sight before opening the door.

"Mr. Lucas Heath, I am arresting you on suspicion of the abduction of Miss Katherine Carter, you don't have to say anything but anything you do say can and will be used against you in the court of law." While DS Williams was speaking, a second officer began cuffing my wrists behind my back.

"No!" I appealed, "You've got it wrong; Kat is special to me, I wouldn't hurt her." I pleaded, knowing even as I spoke the words, nobody is the room believed me. "Kat's the only person in this entire shithole of a town whose ever even given me the time of day, she doesn't deserve to be hurt but it's not me, I swear!" My voice sounding desperate, even to me. I needed to stop talking before I made it even worse. Control yourself, Lucas! If you mess this up, then you and Ethan are both going to pay! I needed to stay calm and see how this would play out, if I don't fuck up anymore then I might still get away without being charged with anything. I can't look after Kat if I'm in prison.

I didn't speak again, instead adopting an almost robotic stature while the officer who cuffed me walked me out of my flat, leaving that main copper and two more searching my things, leading me into the communal hallway and down the flight of stairs. I was still clinging to a last ounce of optimism that this might all still work out ok. Ethan might get spooked by the sudden police presence and run as soon as the chance arises, leaving Kat safe for rescue, and I will be able to lie my way out of all involvement here if I just stay focussed. That last shred of hope dissolving instantly though as I simultaneously heard one officer at the top of the stairs announce he had found the bag I was in the middle of packing and in the same moment saw the door in front of me open, the looks of hurt and horror on the two girls faces cementing to me that I wasn't going to be able to find my way out of this now as all the voices in my head started shouting all at once and everything started spiralling in my mind.

Chapter Twenty-Five

Now

"There's four cop cars out there, look." Sarah hastily called over to Hannah from the living room window, her voice a crackled mixture of desperate hope and panic of the unknown. It hadn't gone unnoticed by Sarah that Hannah hadn't spoken further since she made the connection to Ethan. Sarah had also noticed Hannah repeatedly trying to call Ethan, to no success. "Maybe they're coming to tell us about something they've found thanks to you, Hannah, they've got to be here to say that your help has led them to Kat. It's all going to be ok, Hannah, I promise." Sarah added, running over to hug Hannah. They had only met a matter of hours before, but they were tied together by their mutual love of Kat, and that made them almost like sisters too. Sarah could see the pain and anguish tearing Hannah apart, the protective need to save her baby sister, straining against her loyalty and expected duty to stand by her husband. The sudden weakening of Hannah in front of her eyes filled Sarah will a passion and anger she didn't even know she held.

"KAT!" Hannah suddenly cried out to the ever-thickening air surrounding her, her tear-stained cheeks puffy and her eyes red and sore. "Where the hell are you!"

Feeling her last bit of hope leave her as she imagined her sisters voice calling out to her, Kat felt her body go limp as Ethan secured her newly cuffed wrists tightly above her head. Forcefully ripping Kat's trousers from her legs, causing her to squirm with a fresh wave of unbearable pain, before removing his own, a single tear dropped down from Kat's eye and any shred of fight she had been holding on to trickled away with it.

"Why aren't they here yet?" Hannah suddenly asked, turning her face toward Sarah. "If there were four cars out front, then where the hell are they? They should be banging the door down by now." The hurt and desperation clear in her voice.

Right on queue the sound of a hammering on a door was heard. It sounded off though, too distant for what it should be. With a flash of realisation, Sarah suddenly remembered the envelope she had so urgently returned to show Hannah.

"Fuck, it's him, isn't it? They're here for him, that fucking psycho upstairs!" A fresh wave of hatred heated through her. "I can't just sit and wait any more, I'm going up there, they can arrest me for all I care but that fucking arsehole needs to pay!" Sarah barked, already marching her way towards the door. Opening the door though, she wasn't prepared to be met almost eye to eye with a cuffed Lucas, being escorted though the hall. Without even pausing to think, Sarah swung her arm back and, with a strength she never knew she had, landed a punch hard in the side of Lucas's right temple.

All calm instantly vanishing from his demeanour and seeing red once more, Lucas thrashed to try to break his arms free while shouting a sudden stream of obscenities at Sarah. "Fuck you, you little whore or you'll be getting exactly what's she's getting as well." The evil spilling out through his voice.

The officers instantly flocking to drag him away, down the final flight of stairs, out of the building and in to one of the waiting cars.

Fresh tears evident on Hannah's face as she appeared in the doorway. "What did he mean 'what she's getting'?" Feeling her loyalty wavering as she struggled to accept what deep down, she already knew, Hannah took a deep breath before asking the question she had been willing herself not to ask, "Have you found Ethan yet? I think my husband may have been involved in Kat's abduction." As she said the words out loud, Hannah felt a mixture of betrayal to her marriage and a vaguely familiar sense of determination in herself she had all but lost years before.

Dragging his rough hands across her semi naked body, Ethan smiled to himself that his plan to finally get his revenge on Kat for rejecting him had paid off. She had the softest skin he had ever felt, he couldn't wait to cover it in bruises and mark her as his own. It wasn't his normal approach but something about her just mesmerized Ethan. He was going to take his time and enjoy every moment of this. Transfixed with the vision of her laying there in front of him, helpless and finally at his mercy, Ethan was unaware of the commotion in the communal hallway just a few metres away as he began taking photos of his latest trophy on his phone.

"I know this sounds obvious Mrs Payne, but have you checked your husband's social media accounts? It's a long shot I know but anything that might bring up a location, where he might have been recently. Hannah couldn't believe the thought hadn't occurred to her before now. Grabbing her phone from the sofa she was just sat at five minutes before, Hannah nervously fumbled to unlock it, twice mistyping her lock code before finally accessing what she needed. She began opening all the accounts which led her to feeds from her husband. Bringing up the maps, it was a painstakingly long few seconds wait before his location pinged on to the screen.

"This makes no sense, its showing that thirty seconds ago he was right here." Hannah pleaded to the officer beside her.

"We've already got officers placed upstairs in Mr Heath's residence, there's nobody else there. Another officer is currently searching the rooms here in your apartment, there's no sign of anyone else here either. Is it possible Mr Heath had control of your husband's phone?"

"Well, they own the whole fucking building, don't they?" Sarah cried out, "Seal off the exit doors and search it all, can't you?"

Directing his instructions to the officers scattered around him, DS Williams ordered his team to knock on every one of the six residential doors in the building, if they weren't opened within ten seconds then they were to force entry. With two apartments on each floor, it would be hard for someone to leave undetected. If Ethan Payne was here somewhere then there was no way in hell, he was coming this close just to slip away unseen.

Trying whatever she could to blot out the sickening sensation of her brother in laws hands on her flesh, Kat tuned into whatever sounds and objects she could see or hear beyond this room. She could see out of the window previously covered by the screen but on the first level up and her still being on the floor, there was nothing but distant airplane lights flickering as they went flying by.

She was slowly picking up voices now though, was she imagining them? She couldn't tell for sure but straining to focus on the possible voices kept her body numb to what was slowly happening to her at the hands of her captor. Kat was almost certain now that she wasn't imagining them. Her own flat was right next door, and she was sure she could hear Sarah again. Knowing this was her one and only chance, Kat channelled all the remnants of strength she had left to pull her good leg back and kick Ethan as hard as she could before doing it again, just as there was a banging at the door. Ignoring the sudden knocking, Ethan forced his hand over Kat's mouth while leaning down on her broken leg. The sudden fresh wave of pain from her leg combined with the severe lack of energy she had left making her heavy and weak, the lack of oxygen reaching her lungs now, her mouth covered with Ethan's hand forcing her to give into the wails from her body and let the exhaustion and pain win, her shackled body turning limp as she allowed herself to fade into a blissful state of unconsciousness, just as the door separating her from her saviours burst open.

Chapter Twenty-Six

Six Months later

Sitting round a table in The Wranglers Arms, late after closing, Kat looked up from the hand of cards she was holding and looked round at the faces surrounding her. The boss has instructed them they were to have no more lock ins, but tonight was a special occasion, and Alex didn't need much of an excuse to take it upon himself to break the rules, just this one last time. What's the worst that could happen anyway, Kat had already worked her last shift a couple of days before and tomorrow Alex would be returning his set of keys too, before they all parted ways and headed off down separate paths to begin the new chapters of their lives. Kane's mum was now back in good health, she had found a new man to share her days with, who made her laugh and wanted to help keep her that way, so Kane and Alex had decided the time was right for them to return to their travels round the globe. It had only ever been a temporary home for them, and while they had found friends to care for and share moments with, the itch to get travelling again had continued to build within them both. They had sold all the minimal belongings they had accumulated, keeping nothing but a large backpack and suitcase each, ready to create a new series of memories together. Sarah had given up the lease on her flat too, neither she nor Kat felt they could call it home any longer after the ordeal six months before. The ghosts were too prominent, especially for Kat, plus she still found the stairs hard work with her leg not fully recovered. With a large amount of help from Sarah's dad, the girls decided they needed to escape fully from the memories haunting them in Smith Cove, opting to rent a cute cottage together in a quaint little village near Heslington, where they could start a new adventure and also be nearby to Kat's sister. After everything that happened, Hannah was keen to rebuild herself, wanting to regain more of her true self back and less of the quiet girl always sinking into the background that she had become thanks to Ethan. She had enrolled herself in classes at the University of York, keen to start making a new life for herself. Sarah's dad had invested a year's rent in advance on a little tea shop where the girls could work near their new home. Kat would manage the café side of the business while Sarah could carry on selling her intricate treasures and gifts. It was best for them all. Though they never really spoke further about what they had been through, they all needed closure and a fresh start. Ethan and Lucas were both arrested. Lucas' lawyers were claiming he had suffered some sort of trauma induced schizophrenic episode that he now had no memory of, though that was still up for debate as further investigations found them both guilty of several attacks leading all the way back to when they were first at university together. The sentences hadn't been given yet, but they were expected to be locked up for years to come. It was a happy relief for all involved.

A late-night lock in with a deck of cards was proving to be a much-needed distraction for the friends, even if nobody apart from Alex actually understood the complex drinking game rules he had created.

"Come of Sarah, babe." Alex's jovial voice slurred, "That's a shot for you! Go on my girl, get it down the hatch." He grinned, spilling another shot of tequila into Sarah's waiting glass.

"This game makes no sense." Sarah laughed happily back, before taking her penalty like a trooper and necking her shot in one.

Cheers of drunken encouragement from Alex, Kane and Kat echoed round the empty pub.

"God we're going to miss you boys so much." Sarah announced, still grimacing from her shot. "Make sure you drop in from time to time at our new place when you're back over this side of the equator."

"Of course, we will!" Grinned Kane, "We'll be coming back over Christmas to visit mum, so a few festive bevvies to christen your new place will be a much-needed pit stop for the weekend. That's only, what, eight months away? We will be back before you even get a chance to miss us!"

"Now I'm gonna be serious for a minute here girls, Kane and me love you two, you're like little sisters to us, so please, don't give your brothers anything more to worry about while we're across the globe. Carry on looking out for each other and for the love of God girls, stop bloody inviting strangers into your home!" Instructed Alex, with a tone of humour in his voice but a face filled with worry.

Looking at Alex's serious expression, Kat could see the genuine concern hiding behind the alcohol fuelled speech. For all his larger-than-life personality and constant banter, Alex was just a big softie deep down with a heart of pure gold. Kat smiled to herself and lent over for a hug before telling him he was going soft on them, and it was his turn to take a shot.

"Oh, did you all hear about Jas?" Sarah suddenly announced, keen to lighten the conversation once more.

All eyes suddenly sparkling at the prospect of one last piece of juicy gossip from the dead-end town they were about to leave behind.

"Ooh Sarah babe, I knew you'd have the goods for us, what's our leaving present then, give us the goss!" smiled Alex, laughing along with the others.

"Well, obviously she works in the offy now doesn't she, well I was talking to that other girl who works in there too, Sadie, the cute grungy one and she told me that apparently Jas has been cheating on Jack with her new manager, Sadie caught them at it a couple of times in the stock room, but now she's moving in with him, claiming it's just as friends in separate rooms and Jack's none the wiser!"

"Oh my God!" Exclaimed Kat, before erupting into laughter, "Well, Jack got exactly the drama he deserves with that one, didn't he!"

"Fucking Hell, what a shambles." Alex bellowed, joining in with the contagious laughter surrounding him. "Remind me again why we're all so keen to ditch this shitshow village?"

For the rest of the night the four drank, laughed, told stories, switched to coffee and continued sharing memories once more until the sun started to come up.

"Right, Kat, you get some fresh coffee on, Kane, you chuck us all in some toast, I'll get this stuff cleared up real quick and Sarah, you just sit right there looking pretty." Alex grinned.

"Pretty hungover." Retorted Kane, with an affectionate laugh.

They hadn't planned on a heavy all-night session, but the hangovers would pass, and it was exactly the perfect goodbye they needed to share. They all finished their coffee and toast without hardly saying a word.

"Well girls," Alex turned to them after locking the pub doors one final time, it has truly been a pleasure. I love you both dearly, take care of one another and we will see you again real soon." They all hugged and wished each other well on their new paths before Alex and Kane headed left and Sarah and Kat went right. Ready for wherever their stories took them next. Blissfully unaware of the eyes watching them from a distance.

About The Author

Debbie Mant

Debbie lives in Essex. UK with her husband Brad and their three children.

Nine Lives Of Kat is Debbie's debut novella. Debbie has always enjoyed all aspects of writing, in particular flash fiction and short stories. She wanted to write something bigger, so began creating the story of Kat in her head and first began putting pen to paper whilst on maternity leave with her third child.

Debbie is a keen reader of suspense thrillers, a music fan of all varieties, and a lover of exploring the woods.